PRAISE FOR VIVIAN AREND

"Vivian Arend does a wonderful job of building the atmosphere and the other characters in this story so that readers will be sucked into the world and looking forward to the rest of the books in the series."
~ *Library Journal*

"Steamy and sweet complete with a whole host of colourful side characters and enough sub-plots to get your teeth into. A fab read!"
~ *Scorching Book Reviews*

"There's a real chemistry between the characters, laced with humor and snappy dialogue and no shortage of steamy sex scenes to keep things lively. The result is an entertaining, spicy romance."
~ *Publishers Weekly*

I have honestly waited AGES for Vivian to return to her world of shifters and this new trilogy is just what the Romance Witch doctor ordered! The setting is beautiful, the characters are hilarious, and the best friends-to-lovers story never gets old...
~ *Romance Witch Reviews*

Arend offers constant action and thrills, and her characters are so captivating and nuanced that readers will have a hard time guessing who the villains really are.
~ *RT Book Reviews*

A full list of Vivian's print titles is available on her website

www.vivianarend.com

THE BEAR'S FATED MATE

BOREALIS BEARS: BOOK 2

VIVIAN AREND

This is a work of fiction. Names, characters, places, and incidents either are the product of the author's imagination or are used fictitiously, and any resemblance to any persons, living or dead, business establishments, events, or locales is entirely coincidental.

The Bear's Fated Mate
Copyright © 2019 by Arend Publishing Inc.
ISBN: 9781999495787
Edited by Anne Scott
Cover Design © Damonza
Proofed by Angie Ramey, Linda Levy, & Manuela Velasco

Personal Journal, Giles Borealis, Sr.

I'm not sending my grandsons another note, because I already warned their stubborn bear asses what the rules were, and I don't repeat myself.

I do, however, find as I get older that it's necessary to jot down a few notes to make sure I keep track of all the threads I've got in play. Growing old is a privilege, and a pain—I don't like the alternative one bit, but that's neither here nor there.

For now, I'm going to gloat for a moment, although at my age it's called pride and we'll leave it at that. Tonight was a delight. Never dreamed young James would be the first to get his act together and step up to the plate. Mated at twenty-six! That's the same age I was when I met my Laureen, and it's been fifty-eight years of mated bliss ever since.

James's mate—Kaylee—is a perfect match to his enthusiasm with her quiet, resourceful ways. Knew those two belonged to each other the first time I saw them gravitate toward each other years ago. Friends-first make for the best lovers, or so Laureen has told me over and over again. Who am I to argue with my heart of hearts?

I also know there's another type of partnership that blooms fast and grows strong. If you can't start out friends, good solid enemies are an acceptable alternative.

Alex might disagree with me—

Who am I kidding? Of course, he'd disagree with me because he's a Borealis bear. But I know best. He's not the type to accept a woman who's less than he is. She needs to have brains, brawn, and superior bullshitting abilities.

He needs a woman who's a challenge, and the one I've got in mind fits the bill perfectly. They're a perfect match in all ways, except there's one thing she can do better than him—

Admit she needs help.

No Borealis male willingly asks for assistance. My wife says it's because we're stubborn fools, which is true, but I know a deeper reason. We're not brave enough to let ourselves be vulnerable, not even when we should, and I'm never admitting that failing out loud.

Lara Lazuli is not really in life or limb danger—no way would I stand by and allow her to deal with that sort of nonsense without stepping in, matchmaking be hanged.

No—she's simply about to find herself between a rock and a hard place. She'll figure out the best solution, and my grandson won't know what hit him.

Lara is one hell of a woman. Her wolf is a force of nature, and I bet before Alex knows it, we'll be celebrating another mating in the family.

Although I won't rush him. I've got time off with my own love planned this summer. Of course, Laureen and I enjoying ourselves might *mean Alex filling in for me a few times.* Might *mean he'll have to take my place at events that will put him in the perfect position to rub shoulders with the best thing he's never looked for. Events like the appointment I just tricked him into attending.*

From the way Alex sounded when I spoke with him a few minutes ago, he's already slightly discombobulated. Just the way I want.

No rest for the wicked, my darling mate always says. I'm sure I have no idea what she's talking about.

In the meantime, I have one final letter to send to get things ready for this coming winter and the fall of my final grandson. Then it's up to fate and the mating fever to finish the job for Alex now, and Cooper later.

If I had my way, I'd be in charge of the entire thing, but even at my age I haven't figured out how to mess with Mother Nature. Unfortunately. Think I'd do a damn good job if I were in charge—lock, stock, and barrel!

GILES BOREALIS, SR.

1

July 2, Yellowknife, Northwest Territories

*L*ara Lazuli tilted her face toward the sun and shoved her lingering annoyance away. The sky was clear, the sun was shining, and the motor of her bright red Maserati was purring like the proverbial kitten.

She was determined to appreciate the good moments when they appeared, and with the windows down and warm fresh wind whipping her long silvery-white hair around, this was a good moment.

Focusing on the beauty of the summer day meant it didn't matter that she'd had to put up with all sorts of bullshit at the Orion pack house late last night. Or early morning, to be honest, since it had been nearly three a.m. when she'd finally made it home, only to be shouted at for acting irresponsibly. Didn't matter that at breakfast this morning they had simply picked the theme up again, this time with added nonsense tossed in from her aunt about fraternizing with the enemy.

Her older sister and their aunt were so annoying at times. Crystal and Auntie Amethyst thought they were the cocks of the henhouse—

Deep breath. Deep breath.

Nope, not going there. Today was all about doing something for herself. Instead of protecting and promoting the family diamond business, the class she was about to teach was strictly because she enjoyed the topic, and enjoyed working with beginners.

And who knows? If things ended up going south with Midnight Inc. or the Orion pack, maybe she'd have to look into a new career.

Right now she was expending a lot of energy to fight off the crushing urge her inner wolf had to take her immediate family apart for being jerks.

Jerks, of course, spelled

C-L-O-S-E

L-I-P-P-E-D

A-S-S-H-O-L-E-S.

We could take over, her wolf offered. *Lead the pack.*

Great idea. Which of their throats do you suggest I rip out first? Lara responded. *Crystal is acting like a typical Alpha combined with an overprotective big sister. Not to mention Auntie Amethyst is sure to taste like smoke. You hate smoke.*

Disgusted, her wolf snarled, *We could still do it. Just fast, then eat a good steak.*

Lara snorted in amusement. That other part of herself was always there, always her, and yet distinctly wolf while she was human. The wolf saw solutions in a far more black-and-white light and while there were times she appreciated the reminder to not get too tangled up in details, actual shredding of familial throats wasn't going to happen simply because the matriarchs in her life were beyond annoying.

If they ever crossed the line to dishonesty or cruelty, Lara wouldn't hesitate to fight back.

But that was the kicker—right now she wasn't sure what mischief was going on in the secret back rooms of the Orion pack leadership. For some reason, the highest ranking powers-that-be, a.k.a. Sis Number One and Auntie Number Three, had not yet reopened the doors to include her in their inner circle.

Secretive jerks.

She slowed her car and eased into the parking lot of the high school.

There were many places in Yellowknife big enough to host an information session like the one she was about to present, but most locations had affiliation issues she wanted to avoid.

She could have held the session at the Orion pack's pub, Sirius Trouble, but half her target market wouldn't have come for fear of offending the local bear shifter population. She doubted Diamond Tavern, owned by the highest-ranking polar bears in town, would have allowed her to book space for fear of wolves rampaging in their hallowed halls.

The supposedly neutral convention center was a little too tangled up with sponsorship from *both* Midnight Inc. and Borealis Gems—"the enemy" as her auntie had put it— to work, either.

Jerk.

Her aunt, not the convention center.

The high school, however, was sacrosanct nonaligned territory. Nostalgically, Lara eased her car into the open space where she used to park when she'd attended six years earlier. It was the one time in her life she'd truly enjoyed school because her family had moved to Yellowknife the summer before her grade twelve year, and there'd been no lingering reputations from her older sisters to burn her. Yes, *sisters*—Lara was number five of the bunch.

She stared at the familiar building. Good memories arose of time with friends, although most of them had moved away.

The curse of a northern town. Those who stayed, stayed for good. The rest passed through like a winter blizzard, there for a moment before melting into memory and frostbite.

Enough reminiscing. She was making new friends. She was making a new start, returning after five years of college and tech school.

She grabbed her bag from the back and was ready to step forward when her wolf shot to high alert.

Eyes watching us.

Lara froze then took a deep inhale, checking for a scent. Tilting her head to the side, she allowed the wolf's keen hearing do its job.

The bushes in front of her quivered slightly, and Lara laughed as she met the gaze of the fiercest hunter of the school hallways. "Mac?"

A loud meow greeted her as the oversized tabby magically slipped through the hedge without knocking a hair out of place. He rubbed his flank against her thigh-high red boots.

Lara laid her bag on the ground to free her hands as she knelt to stroke him. "I wondered if you were still ruling the roost. Good to see you, Sir Mac the Magnificent. I assume you've been keeping up on all your superior cat attack moves."

He angled his head to allow her to scratch under his

chin, a purr the volume of a Harley in high gear rumbling from his chest.

Lara scooped him into her lap and hugged him tight, awkward because of the sheer mass of the animal as she balanced on today's moderately sensible three-inch heels.

The rumbling sound strengthened in volume beyond what was typically possible even for a big cat.

That's when she realized someone else had entered the parking lot. Someone on a *real* Harley who was even now skidding to a stop beside her car, dust flying skyward.

She stood, Mac's heavy weight in her arms forgotten, as the man on the bike dismounted and her every sense went into overdrive.

Black leather pants, black leather jacket. Adding those to the combination of black boots, leather gloves, and a mirrored helmet should have made him a mystery, but she *knew*.

She knew far too well.

Alex Borealis loosened his helmet, lifting the gear away then dragging a hand over his military-short dark hair. The sun shone off his square jaw and firm cheekbones, turning the tan of his skin the colour of polished oak.

His eyes fixed on hers, pupils so dark and wide that they blended with his deep brown irises and turned his gaze mesmerizingly dangerous.

Lips. Those gorgeous lips that were firm yet deliciously soft when pressed to hers before hunger had swept in and he'd attempted to consume her—

And that was where her mind was *not* allowed to go. No matter how her inner wolf wanted to lunge forward and complete what had passed between them the last time they met.

Which was...less than twelve hours ago?

Yeah. They had a "history." Short, not sweet, and definitely complicated.

Lara lifted her chin boldly but didn't say anything.

Alex hung his helmet on his handlebars then stripped off his gloves. He unzipped his jacket and it fell open to reveal a black T-shirt stretched over a leanly muscular and extremely lethal body.

Oh, how she wished for the right words to strike him with, but her wolf and her brain weren't cooperating. Instead, the tip of her tongue vibrated with something along the lines of "*Sweet mercy, your place or mine?*"

Her wolf wanted to do it right there in the parking lot, thank you very much.

Alex stepped closer, still staring at her face, as his fingers drifted up to rub his wrists. Faint red lines circled the base of his thick forearms as a reminder that at two a.m. she'd left him handcuffed to a stairwell.

Oops? History again. In her defense, it *had* seemed like a good idea at the time.

"You looking for something, Borealis?" The words rasped out as if she'd taken up her aunt's three-pack-a-day habit.

"Maybe an apology." He stopped a foot away from her, glancing momentarily at the cat. Then, wonder of wonders, a smile bloomed on the bear shifter's stern face. "Is that...Mac?"

Lara slammed her lips together, mostly to stop from drooling. Alex Borealis smiling did something dangerous to her hormones.

Who was she kidding? The damn man could be cursing her name and he'd still do something to her, but that was an issue for a future time. Because, beyond all reason, Alex had reached forward to curl a hand over Mac's head, and the traitorous creature allowed it.

More than allowed—he luxuriated in it, leaning his big cat head into the caress and loudly voicing his approval.

"Two-timing beast," Lara muttered.

Alex grinned harder, lifting his gaze to hers. "We used to spend all lunch hour together, me and Mac."

Which would have been at least a couple years before she'd attended the school. Lara supposed Mac's approval was a point in Alex's favour, but admit it? Hell no. "Yeah? Well, *I* didn't have to bribe him with food to make friends."

Alex rolled his eyes.

His hand slipped off Mac's head and brushed the side of Lara's breast.

Both of them went motionless. He didn't retract his hand—just stood there, touching her. As if he were trapped in a magic force field and not sure how to escape.

Lara closed her eyes and swallowed hard, fighting with everything in her to not follow the damn cat's example and lean into the polar bear shifter's touch.

She knew why it was so addictive, the simple caress of his fingers. The too-close exhalation of air from his lungs across her cheek lit extreme cravings. The urge to grab his massive shoulders and cling tightly as she kissed him senseless was enticing and as desperately needed as her next breath.

Alex Borealis was her mate.

Wolves always knew, which was why, since the moment she'd met the exasperating man, she'd been fighting tooth and nail to keep from jumping his unwilling bones.

Mating was for life. She didn't want *any* man forced to accept her as a partner, especially not one who didn't trust her and thought of her as nothing but an adversary. So, as sexy and desirable and oh-my-God-I-want-him-now as he was, Alex Borealis was off the menu until they could straighten things out.

Noooooooo, her wolf howled in renewed dismay, pain licking along her nerve endings at being denied her mate's caress as Lara forced herself back all of half an inch.

Sorry. Hurts me too, baby, Lara soothed her. *We need to wait.*

Another wave of heat struck as Alex leaned in and his scent drilled through her like a spike.

"*Lara.*" Her name rumbled over her skin, teasing and sensual. It held a touch of awe, as if he wasn't sure what was happening between them but was utterly aware this wasn't a typical reaction between two people who claimed to not like each other.

She was tempted to do something questionable in the pursuit of self-defense when Sir Mac bunched into a tight knot then propelled himself from her arms directly at Alex's head.

2

---

*I*nstinctively, Alex swayed to one side and twisted. His already raised hand allowed him to catch the feline flying at his face and redirect, swinging the oversized missile in an arc and slowing Mac's momentum.

Alex let go, arms pointed toward the parking lot.

Mac did that cat thing, legs flailing rapidly as he twisted his torso to land on all four paws.

The beast gave Alex a haughty glare before stalking off, tail raised high in the air. The very tip twitched as if waggling a finger in pointed disapproval.

"What the hell was that about?" Alex snapped at the annoying, tantalizing, *delectable* siren of a woman who had been driving him mad since her return to Yellowknife three months ago.

He was speaking to empty air.

Lara was marching away from him at high speed, her heart-shaped ass swaying temptingly with every step.

He went after her, his boots smacking into the concrete underfoot with a sharp slapping sound. "I'm talking to you," he all but roared.

Smooth, his bear offered blandly.

Shut up, he told his inner beast.

His bear grumbled back, *It's not nice to shout, especially not at* her.

Alex nearly tripped over his own feet at the vehement tone in the scold. *What's your problem?* he demanded.

His bear went quiet, which was probably a good thing because the rapid march had brought him back in line with Lara, who was fumbling with a key at the school entrance door. The last thing he needed at this moment was his bear distracting him.

Alex placed a hand on the door, leaning over her. "It's not nice to walk away in the middle of a conversation, sugar."

Lara went motionless. He had her caged, his larger body looming like a wall around her. It was a power move, it was aggressive, and yeah, he knew damn well what a shitty thing he was doing.

Although *why* he was doing it, he wasn't sure. There was something about the scrumptious Lara Lazuli that tripped every one of his switches and straight-up pissed him off at the same time.

"You want to back up a couple of paces, *sweetheart.*" Lara's tone was syrupy and polite.

"I want to know where the hell you get off—"

"That wasn't a question," Lara interrupted. "Move now, or I'll move you."

Oh, this should be good. Alex adjusted his stance slightly, noting his previous alignment had left his nuts open to being shoved through his spleen. "That's not very friendly."

"*Alex,*" Lara said, a world of disappointment in her

tone. The bag on her shoulder slipped to the ground. "I thought better of—"

She didn't finish her sentence. Instead, she moved.

He caught a glimpse of what she did, but it didn't make any sense—not unless she'd learned to levitate—because she seemed to walk up the side of the door before flipping in midair to land on his back.

She didn't weigh much, but the momentum was enough to set him off-balance. As he tilted away from the building, Alex scrambled to pull off the same swiveling trick Mac the cat had accomplished. The last thing Alex wanted was to fall and crush Lara under him.

Only, even as he twisted, her weight shifted again and she was twirling around him, catching hold of one of his arms to spin his off-balance torso faster than expected.

He rotated one and half times to land on his stomach, flat on the ground. His arms were spread-eagle, one cheek pressed into the dirt. Lara's knee pinned his neck in place, her other foot planted on the back of his right hand.

That was awesome, his bear said with approval.

Really? For fuck's sake, shut up.

What the hell was wrong with the damn beast? Alex and his internal animal were going to have a long, hard talk about cheering for the wrong side, but that would have to happen later.

For now, Alex ignored the beast and focused on what was proving to be an interesting challenge. "You want to rethink this, sugar? Because I'm willing to take the gloves off if necessary."

She waited. Five seconds, six...

Alex gathered his energy in preparation to move when the pressure eased, and she stepped back, opening a good three to four feet between them. She bent and scooped up her oversized shoulder bag, settling it into place.

Then she took a deep breath, letting it out slowly before speaking. "Maybe we should start again."

Alex stood then brushed the dirt from his knees, meticulously straightening his T-shirt and jacket. His annoyance remained way off the scales for normal, though. He'd deserved to get dumped—he *had* been messing with her personal space.

He glanced into beautiful brown eyes with golden flecks. She seemed to stare at him a little sadly, the way she'd looked at him more than a few times in the past. Her heart was clearly breaking, tugging at previously unsuspected emotional strings inside him. He wanted to sweep her up and protect her. To make her world perfect.

If he gritted his teeth any harder, he was going to wear them down to nubs.

The woman *had* to be the best actress out there. Sad? Needing protection? Oh, please. A month ago he'd watched her effortlessly take down a cougar shifter twice her size.

Something wasn't right, yet no matter how hard he dug, he still had no idea what her endgame was. Only, he wasn't going to figure it out by making demands. This was going to take finesse.

He could finesse, dammit. It wasn't his favourite way to do things, but no matter.

Change of plans. Alex copied her and breathed slowly through his nose for a moment. Each inhale was full of her rich, sweet scent, and a lingering hunger rose in his gut.

He batted down his inner bear, who was humming happily and wallowing in her delicious aroma, and fought to speak as placidly as possible.

"Starting again. Lara, my grandfather had a meeting

scheduled with you today. He can't make it, and he's asked me to take his place."

Her mouth fell open, confusion slipping in too quickly to be an act. "I have no idea what you're talking about. I'm teaching a beginner class for local businesses regarding online security. Why would your grandfather have signed up for *that*?"

"That can't be right." Alex struggled to remember exactly what the old man had told him the previous night. Although to be honest, the conversation had taken place during some rather distracting circumstances. "He said he had a meeting at two o'clock with someone who had cutting-edge information—*you*—and that it was vital I attend."

She dug into the leather messenger bag on her shoulder and pulled out a notebook, ignoring him as she flipped through pages. "Well, I hope it's up-to-date and informative, but I can't imagine Borealis Gems getting anything new from this presentation. Today is all beginner stuff. You've already got the biggest and brightest security available."

"A compliment? Are you sure you want to go that far?" Alex folded his arms over his chest, slightly annoyed at the fierce sense of pride that struck at her praise for his work. Because, as the chief of Borealis Gems security, it *was* his work.

But he didn't need anyone to tell him he did a good job. Certainly not some blonde pixie who seemed to have perfected the ability to get on his last nerve without even trying.

"It's not a compliment when it's true," Lara pointed out, still flipping pages. "In fact, I've heard some of your Remote Access Trojans are still showing up in South America after that hacking attempt last March."

He growled softly, all amusement gone. "How did you know about the RATs?"

Lara lifted her head and looked at him in shock, her fingers stuck between the pages of her book. "It's been all over the news? Every security provider I know is trying their best to duplicate whatever you put in place. It's turned out to be the perfect solution to fend off most hackers because they're scared to death someone will get into *their* systems."

"Oh." The news. He'd stupidly forgotten it was common knowledge and instantly leapt to suspecting she'd been snooping in his business.

The softness that had been there a moment ago melted off her face to be replaced with a strictly professional and utterly unemotional façade. "Yes, *oh.*"

Say you're sorry, his bear instructed firmly.

Alex's back stiffened. He'd been on the verge of apologizing, but now? *Shut up and mind your own business.*

Is my business, you babbling third cousin to a baboon—

Lara lifted her book in the air and interrupted his bear's smart comeback. She pointed to a list of names. "That's weird, but yes, your grandfather signed up for my class. But he only used his last initial, and I wasn't looking at first names that closely. I can tell you right now you don't need to stay. If I offer a more advanced class down the road, you'll have to sign up then. Now, if you'll excuse me, I came early so I could set up before my students arrive."

She turned her back, and there was really nothing he could do except watch as she unlocked the door, stepped through, and firmly closed it in his face.

3

———

With the usual busyness of life, it was nearly the end of July before the weird mistake their grandfather had made returned to Alex's mind. All three brothers were gathered in their retreat room upstairs at the tavern, relaxing and catching up midway through the summer.

Who was he kidding? Everything about that day had lingered in his thoughts far too often. How was it possible to be both intrigued and annoyed beyond measure by the petite wolf shifter? The fact Lara had gotten the jump on him—

Damn it, he was getting a hard-on just thinking about it. Not because he had any particular reason to relish eating dirt, but because it was a turn-on beyond belief to know that as delicate as she seemed, if they ever got physical he'd be able to let go wholeheartedly.

Alex Borealis liked enthusiastic sex.

If he was honest, he also liked how Lara looked. From the top of her silvery hair all the way down to those leather-clad fuck-me boots, she was one hell of a tempting woman.

But what he liked the most was doing what needed to be done for his family, and in his role as chief of security for Borealis Gems, anyone who threatened their livelihood wasn't to be fraternized with.

The other gem company in the territory, Midnight Inc., had been a constant source of annoyance over the years. They'd never done anything illegal as far as he could tell, but there was a constant one-upmanship going on between the two firms. Alex approved of competition in the marketplace, but he didn't approve of people using his family to get ahead, and that was where his main suspicions currently lay.

He wondered if Midnight Inc. was planning on playing dirty. The gorgeous, sensual Lara Lazuli had been slowly making friends with the women closest to his brothers. Women who had access to secrets and the most secure parts of Borealis Gems.

A logical reason for Lara's newfound interest in Amber and Kaylee was to dig up insider information. *That* wasn't happening on his watch, no matter how much her swaying hips made his body ache.

You're grumpy, his bear complained.

I have my reasons, Alex snapped.

Wouldn't be grumpy if you let the wolf pet you.

Alex sighed in exasperation, although he had to agree. A little petting from Lara would do a whole lot to ease his frustrations.

Onto more immediate issues...

Alex tipped back in his recliner with a glass of really good whiskey in hand as he mentioned his current worry. "You think Gramps is going senile?"

A snort sounded, followed immediately by gasps for air. James, the youngest of the three brothers, leaned forward and pounded a fist against his chest, obviously having swallowed wrong.

Cooper eyed him from the comfort of his own oversized leather chair. "I take it that's a no?"

A rasping laugh broke out from James, now blissfully mated to his best friend, Kaylee. "Grandpa Giles might be annoying, but he knows *exactly* what he's doing." James gave one final cough against his fist before examining the swirling amber liquid in his glass thoughtfully. "Maybe we haven't given him enough credit. He's got some good ideas."

"You mean his ultimatum to not avoid the mating fever this year or else? Just because it turned out well for you doesn't mean that's a given for us," Alex reminded him. "Neither Cooper nor I have best friends we've spent years pretending not to be in love with."

A soft shrug lifted James's shoulders before he met Alex's gaze. "I wasn't pretending. I really didn't know. If it hadn't been for Grandpa Giles's edict, Kaylee and I would still be waiting instead of enjoying a relationship that's mind-blowing and life-changing."

The leather creaked on Cooper's chair as he adjusted position, his expression softening. "I take it mated life is going well?"

James's immediate ear-to-ear grin was easy enough to read. "Kaylee's amazing. She's brave, and she's beautiful, and oh my God, the sex is—"

"Yeah, great. We don't want to hear about that." Cooper was the one who said it, but Alex wholeheartedly agreed.

There was nothing worse than having to sit through gloating, especially on their younger brother's part, when neither he nor Cooper was currently attached. And it wasn't as if sex wasn't on his mind...

Go see the wolf, his bear suggested. *She's hot.*

Alex leaned forward and put his empty glass on the table so he could use both hands to rub his temples. *Shut. Up.*

His bear didn't say anything. Just cheated outrageously and sent a vivid mental image of Lara. An instant replay, as it were, of the night he'd stupidly given in to desire and kissed her senseless. Her lips were swollen from contact with his, the buttons of her shirt undone far enough to reveal the top swells of her breasts. Her chest moved rapidly as she all but ate him up with her eyes.

A groan escaped before Alex could stop it.

"Oh, hey. You two had better not be backing out of our deal." Annoyance tinged James's voice. "Just because something unexpectedly good happened to me doesn't mean either of you are off the hook. I was willing to do whatever it took, like we all promised."

Alex lifted a hand to cut off the rant before it went any further. "Not backing out of the deal," he assured his younger brother.

Although Alex was going to do his damnedest to not end up mated, and he was starting to have some wonderfully sneaky ideas regarding exactly how to manipulate the system.

"I'm not backing out either," Cooper assured them both. "To get back to your original question, Alex, I don't think Grandfather is senile. I think he's a sly old fox, but in the end, his wily ways don't change anything. He can't trick his way into all three of us becoming mated this year. If we follow the letter of the agreement, we win. And the only thing he demanded was for us to not avoid the mating fever."

James nodded, pacified by their recommitment. The

three siblings fell into an easy chatter. Just a good time with family and a lot of teasing aimed toward James for having mated with the woman who'd been under his nose for years.

"By the way." James glanced between the two of them. "I'm taking Kaylee with me in a couple of weeks when I head to the London Diamond Festival. We're staying on for a few days to have an actual honeymoon."

"Sounds great. Have fun," Cooper said, a wry smile on his lips. "It's bound to be a whole lot more entertaining than what I'm doing, which is heading south to take a couple of refresher courses and then renewing my law license."

James bumped a hand against his forehead. "That's right. I forgot you were busy. I guess that means Alex is my lucky replacement while I'm gone."

They all helped in different capacities for Borealis Gems, but James handled most of the publicity.

Alex hated publicity work. "You knew you were going to London. Why'd you book something else for the same week?"

"Don't be such a wuss about having to go out in public and smile," James rumbled good-naturedly. "And I didn't double-book, thanks so much for trusting my abilities. I'm booked for an event on October fifteenth that the coordinator suddenly decided we needed to have a rehearsal dinner for on *August* fifteenth."

Alex sighed. "Which means no way you can put them off until you're back."

"None at all. And if you think I'm cutting short my honeymoon because you're feeling antisocial, you've got another think coming." He dug in his pocket and pulled out a business card, spinning it across the room.

Alex caught it in midair.

"Contact information for the coordinator of the event," James told him. "Friday night. Give him a call and see if you're supposed to pick anyone up along the way. I'm not sure who else is invited."

Alex eyed the card. "*Table Talk?*"

A soft laugh escaped Cooper. "Damn. That's one of the hottest programs right now on the Food Network. They're featuring the best eclectic restaurants from around the world. You're going to end up with a fantastic meal, and all you need to do is behave yourself."

"Right?" James said enthusiastically. "Kaylee and I wish we could be there for the food alone, but since we can't, you're going to have to buckle down and do your damnedest to be somewhat pleasant."

"I'm always pleasant," Alex said.

Both Cooper and James paused, eyeing him with identical expressions: slightly amused, slightly annoyed, one brow raised.

"I *am*," Alex insisted.

James's lips twitched. "Except that one time."

"You mean the time he mistakenly pounced on Grandfather's old army buddy?" Cooper said without skipping a beat. "The one who'd trained as a Green Beret and, in one simple move, pinned our boy to the ground?"

"Nope. Now that you mention it, I was thinking of a *different* incident, but that's a good one as well. I was thinking about how the mayor 'accidentally' got locked in a closet, and Alex forgot to tell anyone for three hours because he was sure there was industrial espionage involved." James shook his head. "No, you're right, Alex. I can't think of any possible reason why we would warn you to not be an ass."

Alex glared at both of them, but failed to keep a straight

face. Within moments all three of them were snickering. "Okay, I give you that the one with the mayor was a little over the top, but he *had* snuck into the top drawer of Gramps's desk when he thought no one was looking."

"Smuggling Snickers chocolate bars to a friend when Grandma had the old man on a diet was not a punishable crime," James drawled.

Nope. Alex had blown it on that one, which was why he was determined to not make any more mistakes going forward. "I promise I'll be northern hospitality personified."

It seemed he had some research to do. Maybe he'd watch a dozen or so episodes of the damn TV show to find out exactly what made a person a winner. There had to be some kind of point to the evening beyond shoving food down his gullet.

Because whatever Alex did for the family, he was going to do it right. No way was he going to lose—

Not that life was a competition.

Well, only most of the time. And to be honest, he liked winning. He was good at it. Hell, he did it often enough to be *great* at it.

His bear sent him another dirty shot. The sensation of soft feminine fingers in his hair, sliding down his neck and over his chest. The heat of a soft womanly body pressed against his, her hands doing dirty things to him until the deceitful creature stepped away and left him handcuffed to a railing.

What is wrong *with you,* he demanded of his bear.

The damn beast snickered.

It's not over. She hasn't won, Alex informed the animal.

All his bear did was offer up a happy sigh and a totally nonsensical comment. *I like her.*

Good grief.

Instead of demanding his bear see logic, Alex went with the most mature solution he could think of. He grabbed the decanter off the table and poured himself a triple.

Maybe next week he'd find time to deal with the delectable Ms. Lazuli.

4

---

*L*ara slowed to a stop and perked up her ears instead of rushing forward at high speed like usual. It was already the middle of August, and she still hadn't found anything specific to solve either dilemma—the pack problem or her mate issues.

Frustration was her constant companion.

The conversation drifting from around the corner was quiet enough to raise her suspicions. She pressed her back against the wall and eased closer to the pack office where her oldest sister, Alpha Supreme of the Orion pack, was talking on a phone to someone.

The one-sided conversation was...tantalizing.

"I hate that we have to go so slowly," Crystal complained. "It's not right. But I suppose if the alternative is slashing throats and excessive bloodshed, I can force myself to work covertly for once."

Lara felt her eyes widen. The murmured response was so low that not even her fantastic wolf hearing could interpret it. The tone of voice was reassuring, though, which seemed to work its magic on her sister because when

Crystal spoke again, there was a little less bloodthirsty violence in her words.

"One step at a time. I agree. The best part about this, you realize, is that they're not going to know what hit them once the dust settles. And if we do things right, we'll be able to tie up all the loose ends and there will be no going back. No way to fight what is clearly in all of our best interests."

Whoever she was talking to said something that caused Crystal to laugh, a warm, happy sound that seemed somewhat out of place considering the rest of the conversation.

"Yes, I'm being careful. It's risky, but it'll be worth it. And then all the... Of course. I'll meet you in our usual spot. Watch your back."

The sound of a phone being laid on the desk and her sister pacing the room to settle into her chair were enough to jar Lara from her stillness.

She pulled a pencil from her notebook and deliberately tossed it back down the hallway to make it seem as if she were only now rounding the corner. Lara shifted her feet with increasing pressure as she took her time approaching the office door.

She wasn't the only one with wolf hearing, and until she had more time to ponder it, she didn't want Crystal knowing the cryptic conversation had been overheard.

Lara pasted on a bland expression before stepping into the room and squarely meeting her sister's powerful gaze. "Alpha."

Crystal snorted. "What have you done?"

"Nothing." Lara folded her arms over her chest, her notepad pressing against the crisp cotton of her security shirt. The one emblazed with the Midnight Inc. security logo. "Suspicious much?"

"Only when you come in here and call me Alpha instead of your usual less than hierarchy-based 'Yo, butthead. How's it hanging?'"

Lara lifted her gaze to the ceiling briefly before grinning wide enough to show teeth. "I figured I'd use my best manners since I have a favour to ask."

Crystal rolled her chair away enough to lean back and place her feet on the surface of her desk. "Oh, you're trying to suck up. I approve. Please." She gestured to the chair in front of her desk. "Make yourself comfortable while you grovel."

Mentally, Lara rapidly ran through options. She had a real request for Crystal, a minor one that she wanted to discuss, but in light of the conversation she'd overheard, it might be good to take better advantage of this opportunity.

Maybe being upfront and blunt would help. It's not as if Crystal expected Lara to fawn all over her in the first place.

Which was good, because Lara didn't fawn.

"I wanted you to know I've completed the security review for Midnight Inc. and modernized the few places we had problems. Overall, we're in excellent shape."

Crystal nodded, her gaze hard and assessing. "Done already? Impressive."

"There's no wasted time when you know what needs to be done. We'll need minimal upgrades in the future." Lara placed her notepad on the table, leaning forward in the chair to rest her elbows on her knees. Making every part of her body language powerful and determined, yet not challenging. "I'm ready to become more involved in the pack."

The corners of Crystal's lips curled up slightly. "So eager. I thought when you left town six years ago, you were ready to abandon the Orion pack for good."

"I was eighteen and looking forward to college. I was even more excited to get out from under the watchful eyes of *five* older matriarchs," Lara drawled. "If you remember, everyone was still living at home. You, Auntie, and all three of our sisters."

Crystal snorted. "Oh God, yeah. I'll give you that one. Since taking over after Mom and Dad abdicated, I've only had to deal with Auntie Amethyst hanging over my shoulder and making comments. Things like 'Oh, *that's* a curious way to deal with the situation,' and the extremely judgmental '*interesting*,' and the worst of the lot—"

"That low pitched *hmmm* she does that just screams disapproval, but you can't call her on it because she didn't really say anything?" Lara suggested.

Crystal's eyes blazed. "I hate that fucking noise."

The two of them laughed spontaneously, and hope rose in Lara's gut. *This* was what she remembered. The good times. The connection.

The sensation of nearly equal power. She'd never pushed it, but something inside had always told her that she was strong enough to be Alpha if she wanted it.

Of course we could. Power might be fun, her wolf said with a lazy stretch, flexing her claws.

Fun? A whole lot of work.

At eighteen, she hadn't wanted that kind of responsibility. Now, she'd take it if necessary. She'd do what needed to be done.

Cryptic conversations aside, Lara had always admired her sister...until the rumours had begun. Their parents had left town shortly before Lara's seventeenth birthday, but Crystal had already been in charge for years by that time. Lara had looked to Crystal and Auntie Amethyst for guidance in the rare moments she, as a head-strong teenager, had felt the need for advice.

Now what she wanted more than anything was for all of Midnight Inc.'s dealings to be on the up and up. For the Orion pack to be a rock-solid part of the Yellowknife community.

Her sister swung her feet to the floor and leaned forward as well. "I'm glad to see you're interested in expanding your involvement with the family. I've been thinking about it as well, only I wanted you to dive in and use your training before getting you involved in more pack business. It's been good to have you take charge of Midnight Inc.'s security. It's shown everyone how competent you are."

Lara held her hands palms up. "That's me, Ms. Competent. And I do like my role in security, don't get me wrong, but I feel I'm ready for more."

Trying to tease out an opening to discover what had been going on in the overheard conversation without poking too hard was a delicate task.

There was a reason Crystal was Alpha of the Orion pack—she was strong, powerful, and she wasn't stupid. Lara worked hard to keep her lighthearted and eager expression in place. The last thing she wanted was for her sister to suspect she knew something was going on.

A bloodless takeover...

If Midnight Inc. *was* planning a financial attack on their nearest competitor, getting it accomplished without a physical attack was certainly better than the alternative. Businesses run by shifters tended to break out of the mould when it came to best business practices.

That is, sometimes bills and banking errors were disputed with teeth and claws. Not good for so many reasons.

So, yeah, a legal takeover that was quick and conclusive was a positive thing. On the other hand, Lara had ethical standards she refused to cross. Using underhanded or illegal moves to take over Borealis Gems or put them out of business was a solid *no* in Lara's book.

She'd like to think it wasn't simply because her yet uninformed mate was one of the inheritors to the competition. She'd like to think that it was strictly a moral and upright decision, but Lara realized she was hormonally compromised enough that she couldn't claim absolutely pure motives.

The truth was she *didn't* want anything to hurt her mate, even if she never got around to telling him what he meant to her.

That he was it. The one and only option, forever and ever. Because wasn't that just a dandy thing to inform a person? *Hey, I know you kind of hate my guts, but if you and I don't manage to make this work I'm going to pine after you for the rest of my life. Not only will my heart be broken, but I will never have sex again because you're it.*

Nope. No pressure whatsoever.

"I think we'll be able to use your abilities a little more broadly in the future," Crystal offered, bringing Lara's wandering mind back to the topic at hand.

Lara jerked upright. "I'm ready."

"I'm ready...*Alpha*," Crystal prompted before ducking to avoid the pencil Lara tossed at her head. "I have something in mind. It's a good way to get your feet wet, yet your security training shouldn't be required. Stay alert, though. While I want you to make a good impression, I also want you to practice stealth. If you know what I mean..."

This open-ended hint, offered with a dramatic wink, bordered on the opening Lara needed.

She spoke slowly in response. "You mean that while I'm taking care of whatever task you assign, I should also take an extra hard look around?"

"If it's appropriate, yes. Also, I need you to get a little... *closer*...to people. You need to make sure people trust you. Make friends. That will go a long way at some pivotal moments in the future."

Lara's mind raced with conspiracy theories. This sounded *so* much like the early setup for a takeover. Security skills, stealth. Pivotal moments?

Crystal eyed her. "It's too bad you don't have a mate yet. It would make it easier to...*discuss*...projects with certain influential couples."

What? Oh God, she was not talking about mates with Crystal. Not now. Lara raised a brow as she shoved the conversation down a different line. "Having a mate would also make it difficult for me to get *closer* to other individuals. Ahem."

"Oh. I guess you're right." Crystal waved a hand. "Never mind, we'll worry about that issue later."

Later, as in much later if Lara had anything to do with it. She schooled her features and nodded briskly. "I'll do my best."

---

5

*L*ara stood outside the pack house a few hours later, dressed to the teeth. Her fanciest purse was tucked under her arm as she carefully leaned against the wall and peered at her phone.

While she waited to be picked up for the big event Crystal had assigned her to attend, Lara was holding a three-way text message conversation with the two women who had become her best friends since her return to the north.

Different as they could be, Kaylee and Amber were uber-friends, but they'd willingly welcomed Lara into their tight-knit group.

Kaylee was a Northwest Territory–born bobcat shifter who had recently ended up mated with Alex's younger brother. She was a longtime friend to the Borealis family and now the source of all sorts of interesting polar bear factoids that helped fill a teeny bit of Lara's unmet cravings for anything remotely personal about her mate.

Amber Myawayan was a Japanese-Canadian human who'd come north a couple years earlier looking for her missing brother. The petite human seemed to have zero issues being surrounded by shifters in her role as admin assistant for Alex's oldest brother, Cooper, the acting CEO of Borealis Gems.

The three women had originally banded together over their shared interest in stopping anything illegal at their respective companies. Since then they'd added an even bigger aspiration to their list: to discover the best source of chocolate, at least 90 percent pure, in all its varying taste combinations, that was available by three-day delivery to the north.

Mostly though, they were friends.

Kaylee: *And then Crystal gave you a public relations task? How is PR even remotely related to the hostile takeover of another corporation?*

Lara: *Beats me, but at this point I'm willing to do anything to get my family to spill the beans. It made sense that no one let me know what was going on while I was at school the past few years, but I've been home for six months now. It's time they let me into the backroom conversations.*

Amber: *Well, let's take this as a positive move. I can tell you that Crystal didn't simply make up a job to test your loyalty. Tonight is a big deal, so she's trusting you with a real situation.*

Lara: *I'm not sure how you know this stuff, but thank you? I guess that means I have to actually be nice to people. How weird is that?*

Kaylee: *Stop pretending. You *are* perfectly nice*

Lara: *What I am is looking for the barfing emoji*
Amber: *I agree with Kaylee. You're a great person—who incidentally can knock the knees out from any linebacker who's getting handsy. Honestly, I think you'll be good at PR. Just don't start a fight. Or end one. Or really...try to not use your ninja skills.*

Lara: *I thought you said I was nice! So, you're saying if a "heated discussion" arises during the course of the meal, I shouldn't flip any of my dinner companions to the floor and shove peas up their nostrils? No problem. Let's hope there's no one in attendance who ruffles my fur.*

The little **typing** symbol showed up to indicate that Amber was formatting a text. It sat there. Vanished. Reappeared. Vanished.

Amber: *is typing...*

She was doing it again. Amber had this annoying habit of wanting to share something and then having to reword it fifty million times.

Kaylee: *For God's sake, just spit it out.*

Lara: *What she said.*

Amber: *...*

Amber: *Fine. I was debating whether I should warn you, because no one is supposed to know who else has been invited, but you're my friend. I didn't know what to do with the fact that I was contacted by the organizers, which means*

I know most of the invitees. Alex is going to be there, and that's all I have to say, and good luck, and oh my God, don't kill him.

Lara read the ramble with increasing concern, pausing when she hit the most important detail in Amber's message.

Alex was going to be there.

Great.

Fantastic.

She had no idea what was going on with the Orion pack and now suddenly she was attending some extravagant dinner with Alex where she had to have opinions about the fancy food when all she was going to be thinking about was how much she wanted to climb him like a tree?

Her sister had ordered her to get closer to people. People like...Alex?

Peachy keen, jellybean.

She was about to send off another message when a sleek, black stretch limo pulled up in front of her. The passenger door on the far side opened, a head popped into view, and she froze.

Even pre-warned, the first sight of the bear shifter had her mesmerized. He unwound his long limbs and muscular torso to glide to a standing position. His head pivoted toward her as he made his way around the back of the limo and strode closer like the predator he was.

A very delicious-looking predator dressed in an immaculate black suit with a crisp white shirt peeking out from beneath narrow lapels. His hair was perfection except for one unruly curl that was barely long enough to dip tantalizingly over his forehead. He was clean-shaven, yet the hint of a heavy beard shadowed his firm jaw.

Perfection and desire served up in Armani.

He stopped a foot away, pulling off his sunglasses to let her glance into his deep brown eyes, his pupils visibly dilating as he examined her.

She knew she looked good. Her slinky sea-coloured dress clung to her curves, and her five-inch heels sparkled like stardust. Her long hair was piled on top of her head in a more formal upsweep than the usual ponytail, every inch neatly in place except for the tendrils hanging on either side of her face. Diamond earrings and a simple diamond drop necklace completed her outfit.

His eyes flashed, and a low sound rumbled up from his chest and—damn it—a needy pulse struck squarely between her legs.

Alex drew in a deep breath as if about to say something. His nostrils flared, his eyes widened, and his growl dropped a notch.

She considered burying her face in her hands. Great. He could scent how turned on she was from just looking at him.

"Lara." His voice—pure aural sex.

She stared back, the pulse in her throat beating uncontrollably. "Excuse me."

Lara dragged her gaze away, twisted slightly to put him at the edge of her line of sight, and sent off another message.

Lara: *One of you might want to put an ambulance on alert. I predict somebody's going to get hurt.*

Kaylee: *What? Why?*

Lara: *There's a limo here to pick me up, and it's him—Alex— and he's wearing a suit and even though he's glaring, I just swallowed my tongue.*

Kaylee: *It would be more fun to swallow his tongue.*

Amber: *Kaylee! You want her to get physical with Alex? He's always so uptight and stiff.*

Kaylee: *I'm giggling because I'm twelve. Uptight. Heh. Stiff.*

Amber: *Stop it. No sex jokes. No sex!*

Kaylee: *Why? I mean, why not? A bit of kissing, or more, if the opportunity arises? (Heh-arises-lol!) It's not as if getting together with him would make them insta-mates or anything. Trust me, I know this one. Polar bears are stubborn, and the mating bond requires *both* sides to agree one hundred percent to twue luv 4ever. Remember me doing the Beauty and the Beast magical glowing routine a couple weeks ago once I came to my senses?*

Amber: *We can discuss this more at some future point, but in the meantime, Lara, why are you still online? Don't you have a limo waiting?*

Oops.

Lara tucked away her phone then glanced up to see Alex had folded his massive arms over his chest, thoroughly annoyed at being ignored, which was part of the reason she'd done it.

Better to have him upset than staring at her with sex eyes.

I don't like being mean to him, her inner wolf sighed unhappily.

Just trying to protect ourselves, Lara said.

I know.

Between the two of them, they were hopelessly in lust and nearly frantic for the mate connection to happen. Although that tidbit about kissing and even having sex not being enough to force Alex to mate with her was a juicy bit of intel.

Still, physical contact was dangerous. Extremely dangerous. Even the kind she now faced as Alex held out a hand.

Instinctively, she gripped it, eyes locked on his. Both of them still standing motionless. Wordless.

Because while Lara had been mostly joking in her message to her friends, she also knew the prediction was one hundred percent true.

Someone was going to get hurt, and she was sadly certain it was going to be her.

6

---

*A*lex Borealis was in utter lust.

His bear had gone speechless for once, which was good because Alex had a feeling that if the creature wasn't so floored, he'd be encouraging all sorts of bad behaviors. Terrible, dangerous things like lifting Lara's fingers to his mouth for a sensual lick. That would be followed by a more thorough taste of her skin, up her arm and down her body until he'd found every honey-scented part and made her scream in pleasure.

My God, she smelled fantastic.

The golden glints in her eyes were an echo of the sweetness hovering over her, and at this moment, Alex wasn't thinking about how she was probably up to no good when it came to his family.

He wasn't really thinking about *anything* except how he wanted to take her into his arms and hold her close for a good, long time as a prelude to stripping her out of that dress and taking even longer to enjoy the next stage of the adventure.

Attend a fancy dinner, they said. It'll be easy, they said...

A sharp tug registered on his fingers. "Alex. We need to get going."

Good grief. How long had he stood there in a trance?

Lara edged closer, weaving as if to sidestep him.

No way. Dealing with his inexplicable lust for the woman hadn't been on tonight's agenda, but he was not about to allow her to see him as anything but in control.

He tucked her fingers into the crook of his arm and guided her to the limo door, pulling his charm out of the dusty attic where it had apparently fled.

"Allow me." He opened the door, but kept hold of her hand.

She twisted to delicately place her fine bottom on the leather seat. Five trillion miles of sexy bare legs screamed at him before Lara lifted them daintily into the limo.

That one glimpse was all it took to send all available blood rushing southward. He took his time walking around the vehicle in the hopes the pressure in his cock would ease enough that he could sit beside her without causing permanent injury.

The bit of control he'd regained vanished the instant he opened the door and her scent rushed him.

He didn't have wood, he had concrete.

Still, he settled without looking as if he had an issue in his pants. He knocked on the side of the car to let the driver know they were in position, then leaned back and stretched out his legs.

The car eased away from the curb and Alex turned his attention to Lara. He'd expected her to be on her phone ignoring him or staring out the window. Shockingly, she was doing neither.

She was checking him out. Those golden-brown eyes

stroked him as firmly as if she'd closed the distance between them and used her hands. Her cheeks glowed with heat, but it was when her examination reached his groin and faltered that...

No—

It was *her* tongue darting out to leave a faint trail of moisture that dragged him to the utter edge of sanity.

"Need something, sugar?" His voice was nearly incoherent, it was so deep and husky.

Lara took a deep breath, still staring at him even as she subtly changed position, leaning away from him in the confines of the vehicle.

Her fingers drifted along the hem of her dress.

He wanted to be the one stroking the shimmering fabric and the bare skin next to it. Wanted it so bad he swore his fur was bristling to the surface.

Alex waited, hands resting motionless on his own damn thighs.

The silence stretched between them. His hearing had gone superpowered, and her every shaky breath rasped his body with need.

Finally, she spoke, tilting her chin up. "I'm sorry. I didn't know you'd be attending tonight, or I would have found a way to bow out."

What the hell? "Why?"

Confusion filled her eyes at his one-word demand. "Because it's a special evening with what should be spectacular food, and now it's going to be ruined."

He didn't trust her. He still wanted her more than his next breath. He wanted to know what she was up to. He wanted to take her down on the nearest surface and fuck her until they both passed out from pleasure.

Yup, conflicting emotions ran riotous when it came to

this woman, but it was the unexpected slide of disappointment in Alex's belly that hit the strongest. "You dislike me so much my presence is enough to ruin your appetite?"

Lara's confusion turned to a frown. "Not me, you. You don't like *me*."

She's worried about...you? That means she likes us!!! His bear leapt from A to Z and started picturing them in bed before Alex could protest.

He shook his head to rid himself of the sexual images bombarding his brain. *Shut up now, or I will go on a vegan diet for a month.*

His bear growled.

Only a few feet away from him, Lara braced as if preparing for an attack. "Alex?"

"Sorry. Bear issue. He's being a bastard." He was a little shocked to have blurted out the explanation so quickly.

Understanding and a wry smile softened her features and made her look playful instead of sad. "My wolf does that to me too."

His brothers' command to be pleasant rang loudly in his brain. Along with everything else going on that he didn't understand, the assumption he needed the warning offered a firm place to restart the evening.

He and Lara weren't friends, but he wasn't certain yet that they were truly enemies. Maybe there was a middle ground?

One that involves sex? His bear offered the comment then wisely vanished.

Alex eased forward onto his elbows, taking another deep breath and soaking in her amazing scent. He took one final appreciative glance over her curves before lifting his gaze to meet hers.

"Honest truth? It's not that I don't like you, Lara. It's that I might appreciate your...*assets*...a little more than is appropriate, all things considered."

Her mouth opened in a small O of surprise.

He was going straight to hell for the dirty things he'd like to do to that sweet mouth.

The limo pulled up in front of the Grande Hotel and halted all further conversation regarding his bombshell of a comment.

Alex hurried around to open her door, enjoying her sexy glide to vertical. His bear agreed, rumbling happily as they stared at her legs and the killer stilettos gracing her feet.

His voice came out one step away from a growl. "I'd warn you to be careful on the cobblestones, but I bet you could climb a mountain in those sexy things."

Lara eased closer, politely slipping her fingers around his elbow. "Another compliment. Alex Borealis, if you're not careful, I'm going to suspect you've been kidnapped and brainwashed."

He chuckled then guided her through the mass of people milling around the entrance, drawn by the cameras and lights set up for what appeared to be a film crew.

The main foyer of the building was all rich wood tones and vast spaces overhead, impressive and bold in an overwhelming display of northern architecture. Elegantly dressed couples stood in small clusters as they waited for the organizers to call them into the main room.

A familiar couple stood to one side of the door, chatting with the others. His gramps and grandmother both wore fancy duds and were obviously ready for an evening out.

Confusion struck. The chances of them being here tonight and *not* attending the event? Slim to none. Which meant Alex had gotten all gussied up for nothing, not to mention the lectures he'd endured from his brothers and the sexual torment during the limo ride. Either James had screwed up—not likely—or Gramps had. *Again.*

Fine. Everyone made mistakes, but between this one and the previous one, both of which had sent him on a collision course with Lara, Alex needed to either goad the old man or check closer for the onset of senility.

Distraction arrived in the form of a massive man lingering at the edge of the room. The behemoth seemed familiar, but it wasn't until the man's gaze settled on Lara and narrowed into a glare that Alex recognized him. It was one of the men who'd instigated a brawl at the Diamond Tavern the previous month and come out the loser to Lara's powerhouse skills.

Mr. Troublemaker shouldered forward, nothing welcoming in his approach.

Lara spotted him as well, a soft curse slipping from her lips as she glanced up at Alex. Her expression tightened then seemed resigned. "Play along, please," she murmured a second before plastering her torso tighter against his.

Instinctively, Alex wrapped a hand around her, his palm firmly planted on her lower back. When she twisted, he went with her, and the next moment they faced the belligerent shifter as if a unified front.

Considering the size of potential trouble in front of them, Alex really should've had more of his attention on the man, but the distraction of honey-scented skin was surprisingly strong. The heat and pleasure of contact with her bare skin scampered through him. Desire struck, along with an equal spike of adrenaline. A remote part of him prepared for a fight.

The man was nearly on top of Lara before he stumbled

to a stop, eyes darting to the side to take in Alex. Assessing their close position. Definitely noticing the bared teeth Alex presented in a very fake smile.

The man glanced back and forth between the two of them before offering a frustrated growl. Then sadly, he adjusted course and kept walking out of the group and into the shadows.

Lara let out a slow breath before leaning against Alex. Her lips brushed his ear as she whispered her thanks then added, "I didn't really want to deal with that right now."

Usually he would have felt annoyed at the lack of fight, but for some reason, this time he didn't mind. In fact, if this kept her pressed up against him all night, he wouldn't mind one bit.

Turning back to the room, he discovered a fierce scowl of disapproval on his gramps's face, his gaze fixed on the protective arm Alex had wrapped around Lara—

The scent of her skin drifted through Alex's system and his bear rumbled happily.

Stay with wolf? his inner beast suggested.

Oh, yes, it was a wonderful idea.

The description Giles Borealis had given in passing of Lara weeks earlier came to mind. Gramps had thought the woman was a cold fish and not worthy of Borealis attention? How much would it annoy the old man if Alex stuck to her side the entire evening and showered her with attention?

As a bonus, playing dirty would give him the opportunity to keep a very, very close eye on Lara. That would probably confuse the heck out of her.

Simple and twisted. Perfect. And he could do it all while being as charming and pleasant as he'd promised his brothers he'd be.

A workable plan firmly in place, Alex leaned in close,

his lips next to Lara's ear. "There's delicious food involved, and we both know it's good for our businesses to present a positive face to the world. Under the circumstances, I'm happy to enjoy your company."

7

---

*H*er grip on Alex's arm tightened before she dipped her chin decisively.

He guided them toward the gathering, keeping Lara at his side. The group flowed in different directions as the organizers took control of the evening. And while he lost sight of his grandfather, there was enough else going on to engage Alex's attention.

The banquet hall had been decked out with a number of small round tables with comfortable seating for four. Around the outside of the room, steaming platters of food were being placed on long tables, and the scent rising from them made his mouth water.

Every fifteen to twenty minutes, a small bell rang and everyone rose to their feet and moved to the next table on their personalized list. They loaded new plates with fresh offerings and settled at a different space to converse with new tablemates.

As dinner passed, the good food and good conversation barely dented Alex's awareness of Lara at his side. The scent of her drilled through all his senses. The heat of her touch grew increasingly addictive, and when she laid a hand on his arm, laughing at a comment from one of their companions, Alex had to acknowledge he wasn't suffering in the least.

It wasn't until the final rotation that they ended up matched with his grandmother and grandfather.

Time to act it up.

Alex pulled out a chair next to his grandmother for Lara. He leaned in and pressed his lips gently to her cheek. "Relax, sugar. I'll get us another drink."

Her eyes flashed with something that might've been a warning, but she kept smiling. "Thanks, *sweetie*. This is the perfect opportunity for me to ask your grandmother some questions."

Drat. Leaving the two of them alone together wasn't necessarily the best idea, especially since his gramps was nowhere in sight.

But Grandmother Laureen waved him off. "Go away, Alex. Lara will be fine with me."

When he hesitated, she raised a brow, her iron backbone showing itself clearly even as she smiled demurely. The woman had put up with Gramps for umpteen years. Stood to reason she'd be as stubborn as any of them.

Lara pursed her lips and teasingly blew him a kiss. Alex rolled his eyes good-naturedly as he stepped away from the table to get them drinks.

He'd just picked up two fresh glasses of an excellent Merlot from the wine bar when he turned to discover he was on the receiving end of a very disappointed gaze.

"What are you up to, boy?" Gramps demanded.

Playing ignorant was so satisfying. "Six foot four."

The furrow between his grandfather's brows deepened

as he glanced back at the table where Lara and his grandmother were chatting. "Care to explain what you're doing with *that* woman?"

"I thought you admired her? Said she was a security expert?" It was fun to toss the old man's words back at him.

A rude noise escaped his grandfather. "I said she was the only one of a bad lot with anything approaching a brain, but I was talking about business, not pleasure. The woman is all wrong for you. Ridiculous to see you hovering over her. She's playing you, I tell you. Certainly would never be interested in your type, and good riddance."

"*My* type?" Alex wasn't sure if he should be amused or annoyed. "I'm a fine type—unpredictable. And of course she's interested in me. I'm a Borealis."

"Balderdash! Pretty, I'll give you that, but a cold fish. Smart mind—good with security, obviously—but nothing there to heat up a man and keep him happy." His grandfather paused, understanding brightening his face as he nodded decisively. "Oh, I get it. You're obviously doing your duty for the company. Brilliant idea. I appreciate it. Painful you have to put up with her, though. Don't go overboard. Makes you look silly, fawning over someone so clearly unsuitable."

Sheer anger shot through Alex. First, he didn't look silly, and second...what the hell was wrong with his grandfather's eyesight? Was he going blind as well as senile?

Cold fish? *Lara?*

His response came out far icier than he'd typically use with the family patriarch. "How about you take care of your wife and I'll do as I damn well please?"

"Watch your manners, boy," Grandfather Giles scolded him sharply.

Alex bowed slightly. "Of course. If you don't mind?"

Before the old man could protest, Alex added the wine glasses he held to the tray Grandfather Giles was balancing. Then he turned on his heel and marched double time back to the table, leaving his elder to move more cautiously as he struggled to keep everything vertical.

He leaned in to press a kiss to his grandmother's cheek. "Have you been taking good care of my Lara?"

Grandmother Laureen blinked at his casual claiming, but less than a second later her smile widened to include Lara as well. "It's been lovely. Did you know she went to my alma mater for college?"

"I did not know that." Alex caught Lara by the hand and tugged her to her feet just as Gramps arrived rather red-faced and puffing from having to dodge others to get to their table. "Excuse us. I need to speak with Lara privately."

"It was nice to meet you." Lara had to toss the comment over her shoulder as Alex kept a firm grip on her wrist and all but dragged her toward the side of the room. "Alex. Slow down."

They were drawing attention, which was pretty much what he wanted. "I need your help," he told her bluntly. "Play along."

Maybe the repeat of her order from earlier in the evening helped. Her demeanor changed instantly. Instead of fighting him, she flowed at his side, strong and delicious, like honey-scented danger.

"What's wrong?" she asked quietly, scoping out the area like the trained security expert she was.

There. A few feet before them was the storage room the extra chairs had been brought out from earlier.

Alex twirled Lara then used his body to press her backward until she was pinned by him to the solid wood surface. Gloriously soft curves and heavy breasts meshed against his torso while lust shot through his system.

"Don't hit me," Alex ordered. "And don't wiggle. I need you to kiss me. Right now."

Her gaze darted over his shoulder, and for one split second he wondered if she would call his bluff.

Then she leaned in and pressed her lips to his. Her hands wrapped around his shoulders, fingernails digging into his muscles. Enthusiasm and fire burned in her kiss as if she'd been waiting her entire life for this opportunity.

The desire to tease his gramps changed to driving need.

Alex cupped the back of her neck with his right hand and dove in one hundred percent. Her taste rushed him, her torso shifting slightly against his in a way that made it impossible for her to miss the two-by-four rising beneath the front of his dress slacks.

Behind them, muted conversations continued as most of the room carried on devouring the delicious tidbits. But his gramps was watching; Alex was sure of it.

Good. Cold fish, indeed.

He twisted the door handle, catching Lara before she fell then following her into the darkness.

"What—?"

The door clicked shut, and her question was swallowed by his mouth as he went back for more. He'd unleashed the beast, and while they wouldn't go *too* far, stopping now...?

No way. Not unless she called him off.

Thank fuck Lara seemed to have no intention of making that call. She was the aggressor, and even with her wolf claws in, she still scratched his shoulders hard enough to leave stinging lines of pain as their tongues tangled and hungrily fought for more.

She rubbed against him, moaning in frustration.

Alex slid a hand down to tug her dress high enough he could catch hold of one leg and hitch it over his hip. The heat of her core pressed to his groin, and only the knowledge that there were people, including family, outside the unlocked door stopped him from shoving open his zipper and taking her right there.

"*Yes.*" Her enthusiastic moan rippled over his skin in a wave.

Her head dropped back, and he pressed his mouth against her neck, suckling hard enough to leave a mark. This was madness, it was impossible, but as he rocked, fire building up his spine, the coming explosion was inevitable.

He twisted his hips, adjusting enough to make perfect contact with the heat of her core. Slowing now, he moved deliberately. Rubbing them together in a steady, demanding rhythm that left her quivering under his grasp.

"I... Oh, *my—*"

"Say my name," Alex demanded. He caught hold of her earlobe with his teeth before sucking it into his mouth. A low keen escaped her lips. "*Say it.*"

How she'd understood him, he didn't know. His words had been nothing more than a guttural growl, but the next thing he knew she'd shoved one hand into his hair and pulled his head back far enough to look him in the eye as she breathed out his name in about twenty-seven syllables.

"*Alllleeeeeeeeexxxxxxx.*"

He crushed her mouth under his, drove his hips faster, and as she broke apart in his arms, he captured her cry with his lips then joined her in release. Pleasure streaked through his system hard enough his legs were on the verge of collapse.

His weight against her was the only thing keeping her vertical, and their rapid breathing echoed in the small room.

Satisfaction, yes, followed instantly by the desire for more, and there in the darkness, Alex laughed softly.

Lara stiffened under him. He murmured soothingly as he offered a soft nudge with his nose along the smooth side of her neck. "Not laughing at you, sugar. Just thinking my brothers told me to be on my best behavior tonight. I'm trying to decide if they would rate this a plus or minus, because I sure the hell tried my best, considering the circumstances."

She snorted before coughing daintily. "My sister told me to make friends. I don't think she meant friends with benefits."

He chuckled again. "Who knew that the two of us could be so cooperative?"

Truth.

They pulled things together and straightened themselves up in the darkness. Alex was thankful for his bear-sized pocket handkerchief to deal with the mess, but he couldn't stop grinning. It was clear that some of the tension between them had faded. He still didn't trust her—not completely. But he was more willing to take a chance and see exactly *what* she was up to before judging her dangerous.

Because one thing was certain—there needed to be more of *this* headed into the future.

8

---

*L*ara rubbed her temples, willing the ache to subside. Her entire body was on pins and needles, and her wolf was ready to go feral.

It had been five days, twelve hours, and fifty-seven minutes since she last saw Alex—in passing, at the grocery store. And she'd come *this* close to tackling him to the ground and stripping him right then and there.

Five days, twelve hours, and fifty-eight minutes.

Yes, she'd been keeping count and wasn't embarrassed in the least by that fact. Timing it gave her something solid to think about, and that meant she wasn't slipping outside to shift to her wolf so she could track his ass down to get what she really wanted.

That sexual experience in the dark a week earlier had opened a door better left closed, and now the cravings were getting worse.

The only way to get through this impossible situation was distraction and routine. She picked up the mail she'd grabbed from the pack's post office box, stacking the pile neatly on the left side of her desk.

Letter opener in hand, she slit open the first envelope, working hard to not imagine running that blade along the front of a certain Alex Borealis's shirt. With her mind working overtime, she pictured buttons flying everywhere before the freshly pressed material parted to reveal his lickable chest—

The letter opener slipped, jabbing her ring finger. Lara cursed, and shoved the punctured digit in her mouth to soothe the pain.

Great. Fantastic. Peachy keen, and awesome.

Now she was not only hurting because she wasn't allowed to touch the man, she was hurting herself while *thinking* about touching the man.

For the next fifteen minutes, she willed her wolf to behave so she could concentrate enough to keep at her task. Bills in one pile, correspondence for Midnight Inc. in another. Junk mail to be recycled in the third.

She was nearly done when a gold envelope revealed a simple three-by-four-inch cardboard voucher.

Congratulations!
You're this month's recipient of an all-inclusive, three-night
stay at

Shimmering Delights

Our world-class spa and retreat centre is delighted to welcome you. Prepare to be immersed in pleasure. Please contact us to arrange your date of arrival and the bonus relaxation packages that suit you best. We look forward to hosting the most memorable weekend of your life.

Lara stared at the card. She read it again.

She picked up the envelope—addressed to Ms. Lazuli of Midnight Inc. The only other details were on the back of the card. The usual fine print disclaimers regarding no cash equivalent, the prize must be taken as presented, yada, yada, yada.

She typed *Shimmering Delights* into a search engine. Two minutes into perusing the website, she was drooling. It was not only a real place; it was the closest thing to heaven on earth imaginable.

Only...

Was the certificate for Crystal or for her? Why was this in the Orion pack mailbox without a specific name? More importantly, was the spa *really* a spa, or a front for something more nefarious? Money laundering. Smuggling.

Suspicions rising, Lara phoned the number on the card.

"Shimmering Delights. This is Vanessa, how can I make your day more enchanting?"

Lara jammed her lips together to stop from snickering. Okay, they were right on brand but still... "I'm trying to track down if this is a real gift certificate or fake."

"I can definitely help you with that," Vanessa said, reassurance and soothing calmness in her tone. "If you could check on the back side of your card, upper left corner, there will be a six-digit alphanumeric code."

Lara flipped the card over, astonished to discover a code exactly where Vanessa described. She read it out loud.

"One moment as my system brings up the information."

Waiting patiently was not Lara's strong suit. Not with her entire system buzzing with need.

Thankfully, Vanessa reconnected a second later. "Do I have the pleasure of speaking with Ms. Lara Lazuli?"

Aaaand Lara was back to being suspicious. "How do you know that?"

"The information I have on file for that code says you are the recipient of a Weekend Indulgence package. Data also tells me you entered for a chance to win six months ago while attending an open house in Toronto. The Futures in Tourism event."

Wow. This was legit. Lara clearly remembered wandering that fair and stuffing her name and contact information—via Midnight Inc. for security purposes—into every prize box possible.

She blinked a few more times then allowed happiness to grow. "Well, I guess that's actually me. Go figure, I won something other than a stuffed bear at the country fair."

"Wonderful. Then shall we select a date for your trip to Shimmering Delights?" Vanessa returned smoothly. "We're booking right now for next March."

Oh my God, *no*. That was seven months away. No way would she last now that the possibility of massage and hot tubs had been offered.

Before Lara could speak, though, Vanessa perked up.

"Hang on. I see there's been a cancellation for this weekend, starting tomorrow. It's for the Grand Salon. I can't imagine anyone else will book on such short notice. I can offer an upgrade if you're interested. No charge, of course. Does that work?"

Lara would make it work. She dashed the date across the bottom of the card followed by a series of exclamation marks. "I'll be there with bells on."

A soft chuckle carried over the line. "If that makes your weekend plans better, I encourage you to do so. I'll email the information you need. We look forward to seeing you for the best weekend of your entire life."

The bloom of happy energy inside was impossible to contain. Lara hung up and hit her feet. She did a victory dance, bouncing around the room and letting her tensions ease away. She still didn't have a clue of how to deal with her craving for her mate, but a weekend of massages and indulgence would go a long way to temporarily easing her pain.

Jeez, her cravings for the man were so bad she could swear she scented him on the air. His rich masculine aroma was doing terrible things to her insides and the space between her legs.

Why is he here? her wolf demanded. *Want him.*

It's our imagination, Lara assured her.

Oh, please. Which of us has the better sniffer?

Good point. If it wasn't her overactive imagination, then Alex was not where he should be—she couldn't imagine any of the Orion wolves allowing him to take a tour of the pack house.

She flew across the floor to the door as if shot from a bow. Slowly, slowly, she poked her head around the corner in the hopes of catching him in the act of trespassing.

The hallway was empty except for that addictive scent.

Ten feet away near where another hallway joined to this one, a faint shadow that seemed out of place stretched across the floor. Lara eased forward, ready to leap on whatever lay just out of sight—

Behind her, a loud clatter split the air, as if something heavy and metallic had hit the floor. Lara's attention instantly shifted to the south.

"Dammit, *help*. Lara. Crystal. *Anybody*." Auntie Amethyst cursed again then fell silent.

Lara headed at a full run to rescue her aunt, the tantalizing mystery regarding Alex temporarily pushed aside.

9

Breaking and entering was such a strong label, with such negative connotations, for what could be considered simple information gathering. Besides, as Alex continued his rapid mental justification, he *hadn't* broken in. He'd walked into the pack house—

Okay, he'd climbed a back wall, crossed the roof, and slid into the ventilation system before ending up in the remote hallway he'd *then* walked down to get to this point.

See? No breakage. A simple stroll, really.

Technically, sneaking wasn't even illegal if you were doing an "I'm here to check out your security systems for a friend" kind of thing. Of course, *that* sort of arrangement was usually set up in advance between two parties, but checking with Lara to see if she was interested in his expertise seemed a moot point.

She *had* admired his large, impressive Trojan before, after all. She had to approve of his checking out her...systems.

His bear snickered in anticipation. *May I make a joke? That it's large and impressive?*

Oh, please. I'm *large and impressive. I meant your supposed expertise. If you're talking about sex, don't you have to actually practice to stay at the top of your game?*

Shut up, Alex responded out of reflex, but he was mostly amused. It had been a dry spell lately.

Just saying...

Alex grinned. He slipped farther down the hall then slid through the open door leading into the Orion pack office. It was too easy—made easier by that call for help he'd heard.

For a second he'd braced himself to respond, the fact he was in the pack house illegally totally irrelevant, when the sound of laughter followed immediately from the same direction. Obviously the issue had been easily dealt with.

He eased the door shut, noting there was no lock. Pretty much as he'd suspected. No wolf in their right mind would dream of entering the Alpha's domain unasked.

But Alex wasn't a wolf. He was a growly polar bear who was fed up with his lack of information. His searches were getting him nowhere, and other than the occasional glimpse of the woman, Lara wasn't cooperating by hanging out where he could stalk—*track* her easily.

Something was up, and he needed proof. Breaking into —wait, he was calling this a security run, not a B&E —*checking out* the pack house was strictly a matter of information gathering.

He needed to know more, and nothing else was working. Time to take his destiny into his own hands and all that stuff.

An unexpected rush of heat swamped him, and Alex wrapped his fingers around the edges of the desk to catch his balance. Lara's sweet scent grew stronger. He closed his eyes and all but groaned as lust roared through him.

Lust and aching physical need.

Want. Want now.

All the joking from a few moments earlier was gone from the beast's tone, leaving nothing but pure animal need. Which was...

Unusual.

Alex pressed his palms to the solid wood surface and quickly considered the facts. His bear was usually vocal, but in an annoying-but-you-know-I'm-a-beast kind of way. The only time that changed was—

Oh shit.

Want sexy woman. Want wolf. Need *wolf.*

Alex scrubbed a hand over his face. The only time his bear got like this was—

He nudged his inner beast. *Are you saying what I think you're saying?*

A low growl of demand was the only response. Which was typical headed into this situation.

Great. Number one reason for this kind of behavior: mating fever was closing in.

The calming breath Alex attempted to take backfired as a full-on rush of Lara's scent rolled into his nostrils and left him shaking with need.

Think. He had to *think.* If things progressed as usual, the urge to fuck would fade slightly then return, a little like a rollercoaster, for the next twenty-four hours. After that, there would be no stopping the animal instinct to mate, and the drive would continue on high for a good solid week.

After seven years of dealing with the fever, Alex had a well-established routine. When he reached this point, he would pack a bag and head into the wilderness to hide out for the duration, avoiding contact with anyone of the opposite sex. With the promise he'd made to his brothers and Gramps, that option was unavailable.

But he'd been strategizing ever since his brother James had mentioned his plan to deal with mating fever had been to track down his best friend and switch up their relationship to include hot fucking.

Alex had no intention of imitating the second part of his brother's plan, which had ended up with James actually mated with his fever partner, but the basic premise was brilliant.

Find someone Alex's bear wanted to get cozy with who was not otherwise compatible as a mate. Someone like the dangerous yet sexy Lara.

Did he want her in his bed? Hell yes. And not only there... He wanted her under him on the floor, and against the wall, and in the shower, and riding him like he was a goddamn pony.

Want her forever? Hell no.

He didn't trust her, but that didn't mean they couldn't connect all the right circuits for one explosive week.

More time before the fever struck would have been nice, but the rush of need in his belly said he simply had to deal. So be it. What he needed to do was track down Lara then convince her that wild and dirty was vital to both their interests. Or at least both their libidos.

He knew she lived at the pack house, so he'd have to entice her away for the week. Maybe bring along a few incentives like chocolate and really good doughnuts, but after the heated passion they'd shared in the closet, he figured there was at least a chemical attraction to sweeten the idea.

Turning toward the door to sneak away and begin the next part of his plan, Alex caught a glimpse of a paper lying on the desk. Lara's scent was all over it, her handwriting in the bottom corner.

Sheer delight rose as he examined the information, especially the part that noted a date at the spa beginning tomorrow and going on for three nights.

A wicked, wonderful idea struck. He didn't need to convince her to come to his apartment. She already had the perfect mating fever getaway location organized. Brilliant woman.

Sexy, sexy wolf, his bear moaned.

For once, Alex had zero intent of telling his inner beast to shut up. But it did remind him there was a point he needed to emphasize. To be certain his bear was on the same page.

We can track down Lara, but you know what we do with her is just for fun.

Excitement rang clearly in his bear's mental tone. *Seriously? I get to play with sexy wolf?*

There we go. Playing and fun and full-on frantic sex were all one and the same, and knowing that his bear was on board with that was fan—*fucking*—tastic.

We get to play if she says yes, Alex warned.

Because as much as he'd be going mindless with mating fever, he wasn't an asshole willing to take an uninterested woman. If she said no, he'd be out the door and headed into the bush in his bear form to suffer alone. Screw the pact he'd made with his brothers—if he couldn't have Lara, he wasn't going to go find a random hookup.

The thought of being with another woman made his skin crawl.

Lara saying anything but yes became even more important. *We might have to get creative when we ask her.*

I will take care of that. I'm far more charming than you, the beast informed him jauntily.

Alex laughed softly as he made his way back to the roof of the pack house. The fresh air hit his face, sharpening his senses and brightening his spirits while he snuck away.

He stopped at his personal office to finish up a couple of vital tasks, slipping away an hour later with the happy sensation of starting a holiday. Which was a wildly different mind-set than how he usually felt at this point of the mating fever adventure.

He was headed to his apartment to pack a bag when an incoming call clicked through his hands-free phone.

Call from: Gramps.

Since the night of the gala, Alex had successfully managed to avoid the old man outside of business hours. No way did he want his gramps to know what was going on right now, either, since most of the messages on his answering machine involved the Borealis patriarch berating him for wasting energy on Lara.

Still, maybe before disappearing for a week he should do a little damage control to keep the old man off his scent. "Hey, Gramps. How goes the day?"

"My day is fine, but there's obviously something wrong with yours," Grandfather Giles complained. "Why am I leaving voice messages for you when you never return them?"

It was too much to resist. "I don't know. Why *are* you leaving voice messages when I never return them?"

His grandfather growled. Alex barked out a laugh.

"Ungrateful cub." Gramps clicked his tongue disapprovingly. "You are rather brilliant, though, so I'll forgive a few little foibles like you forgetting your manners."

"Thanks so much. It's good to know you think I'm

brilliant, although I'm not sure what brought that on." Alex transferred to his phone as he left the car in the parking lot and headed up to his apartment. "Anything in particular?"

"Keeping an eye on that undersized woman from Midnight Inc. was smart. I like your initiative, although it would've been nice if you'd warned me the cozying up last week was all a job. Had me worried you were losing your senses for a while."

Once again Alex wondered about his grandfather's mental health. "Anything in particular about Lara give you pause? Anything concrete for me to trace, that is."

Because random comments about how unsuitable and impassionate she was made no sense and just annoyed his bear.

"Woman can't look me in the eye. Never trust a person who can't fix you square on in the eye and give a polite hello," his grandfather warned as if Alex were a preteen learning public etiquette.

"When did you last see Lara?" Alex didn't remember his grandfather meeting her other than briefly at the gala.

"Five minutes ago. I was in the grocery store picking up a few things, came around the corner, and she was there pushing a cartload of junk food and ice cream."

Unexpected food choices, and ones that his time with their office manager, Amber, told him Lara was looking for some comfort. Or she had a sweet tooth.

The things he didn't know about her nagged like a sore tooth.

"Since when did you become a Canada's Food Guide critic?" Alex asked his grandfather. "I seem to remember more than one bag of Halloween candy stashed in your office over the years."

His gramps grumbled good-naturedly then tossed out

the lulu of all suggestions. "I think she was heading out on a road trip. I might've eavesdropped a little, but it seems the woman is driving north in the morning. I don't like the sounds of that, my boy. You have anything dire at the factory in the next while that you can't put off?"

It was an unexpected answer to one of his problems. "Are you telling me to follow her?"

"I wouldn't presume to tell you how to do your job, but considering we have holdings to the north and Midnight Inc. doesn't, her trip strikes me as suspicious. Might be a good thing to keep an eye on her." His grandfather had dropped to a quiet, conspiratorial tone. "Always better to keep ahead of the competition. Get a jump on them, so to speak."

A violent ache shot through his gut as his bear offered a picture of Alex jumping on Lara. Both of them naked.

Alex gritted his teeth as he fought for control.

His voice still sounded raspy when he managed to answer. "Thanks for the heads-up. I won't be in the office for the next few days. Depending on what happens, I won't be answering my phone either. Don't worry. I've got this under control."

His grandfather answered politely, and then they both hung up.

Alex had to admit, at least to himself, that while it was the perfect solution to getting out of town and dealing with the mating fever on the sly, he'd totally lied his ass off.

Under control? He was the furthest fucking thing from it.

10

_____

*L*ara lay on her back on a cloud of softness, relaxing in front of a roaring fire. The rug under her was made of something fluffy and was so sensuously addictive she couldn't stop stroking it. Soft music played, turned on with a simple verbal command.

The lighting was low, and the scent of ripe strawberries hung in the air. They were one of the delectable items in the loaded dish of fruit and chocolate that had been waiting for her in the room.

Room? No, this place was bigger than her apartment, and she already knew leaving in three days would be tough.

The drive had been short, and checking in to Shimmering Delights had been remarkably like what she imagined living as royalty would be. Escorted through the main entrance and directly to the suite, she watched as people in uniform appeared and disappeared rapidly. Everything that she needed was within calling distance as luxury screamed out at her.

The only thing wrong was the aching hole inside her that longed to be filled by the company of her mate.

We'll make a plan, she promised her wolf. *As soon as we get back, I'll go to Crystal and find out what's going on.*

Because once she knew for sure, she could take steps to maybe approach Alex. Maybe try to broach the idea of something more between them—

Lots between us, her wolf commented dryly.

Lara's instant mental image of having *nothing* between them was sheer torture. She'd had his body against her now. Heck, she'd had her hands on his body, felt the heat and strength within him.

She found herself stroking the blanket, cursing softly at the realization each stroke reminded her of teasing her fingers through Alex's hair.

Pounding need struck.

Good grief. Here she went again. Lara sighed as she slid a hand under the waistband of her pants, slipping her fingers between her legs.

The images weren't going away, so she might as well indulge in a little pleasure-induced relief before the warning timer she'd set went off for her first spa session.

She'd gone for sheer comfort for her getaway. With no plans to go out in public the entire time, her clothing had all been pulled from the favourite part of her closet. Her current apparel was her oldest pair of pyjamas, faded and baby soft and worn so thin that she needed the heat from the fireplace to stay warm.

Or at least she did until she pictured Alex beside her. His dark eyes fixed on hers as he undid the buttons of his shirt and let it fall to the ground.

She'd felt his muscles under her fingertips. Felt the flex and power as he'd held her close. Felt the tremour in his core as she touched him, and she took the sweet delicious sensation in and imagined him curling himself around her.

Resting his hands on hers and following along as he learned what she liked. Slow caresses, building pressure.

She moved her legs slowly against the soft caress of the carpet, adding layers of pleasure to the heat building in her core. Moisture covered her fingers at the thought of him working his way down her body. Hands pressing her thighs apart to expose her most intimate center.

Her legs quivered, tension spiraled, and dream Alex leaned in, mouth covering her sex as his tongue—

A firm knock rattled the door.

Lara's fingers faltered for a stroke then picked up again. She ignored the summons. She wasn't expecting guests, and there was nothing she needed to do more than deal with what she was doing at that moment.

Instead of his mouth, she wanted his fingers. Pressing inside slowly, slicking over the—

Bang, bang, bang.

Lara groaned in frustration and rolled to her side. She stumbled to her feet, tugging her pants into place.

Open the door, her wolf ordered eagerly.

What are you talking about? Lara demanded with annoyance as she put her eye to the peephole.

It's him, her inner beast informed her as Lara's eyesight confirmed the impossible truth.

Alex Borealis stood in the hallway, staring at the door with fire in his eyes.

Oh. My. God.

Maybe if she ignored him, he would go away.

Noooooooooooooooo. An easily understood sentiment from her wolf.

In the hallway, Alex straightened, unfolding his arms from where they'd lain across his chest. "Open the door, sugar. I know you're there."

The words came out quiet but forceful. Demanding, as if he could order her around, and suddenly her temper flared.

Lara jerked the door opened and glared at him. "What the hell are you doing here?"

He took a deep breath and his nostrils flared. A shudder quaked through him. He closed his eyes, and every muscle tightened as if he was fighting an internal battle.

Then he straightened, his gaze locking on her eyes. "Christ, woman. You're killing me."

He knew. Lara licked her suddenly dry lips because it was clear he knew exactly what she'd been up to a moment ago. "What do you want, Borealis?" she demanded.

His gaze dropped to the floor briefly before he lifted it, this time without the demanding attitude and with one hundred percent truth held up like an offering. "You. I fucking want *you*."

It was the last thing she'd expected to hear. Suddenly it was hard to think, considering the calisthenics her wolf was doing inside her brain. But she was pretty certain what he was saying and what her wolf wanted to hear were not the same thing.

The sound of voices down the hallway announced they were going to have an audience within seconds, so Lara did the only thing possible. She caught hold of his shirtsleeve, pulled him into the room, and closed the door firmly behind him.

"This is not me agreeing to anything," she warned. "This is me trying to deal with what the hell is wrong with you without witnesses."

Alex went surprisingly meek for a moment, marching at her side to what should be the safest place in the suite. Only, as she reached the kitchen and twisted to discover his gaze had been fixed on her ass, the truth was at this particular moment neither of them seemed to have full control of their brains.

She folded her arms over her chest. "Ignoring bigger questions such as how did you know I was here and what kind of creep follows a woman to her hotel when he's not invited, I want to know what you mean by that outrageous comment."

Alex caught her hand in his, tugging it toward him. He swore softly, eyes blurring for a second as he lifted it to his lips.

She should've moved sooner, because when he opened his mouth and sucked her fingers into the wet heat, she couldn't move. He closed his eyes and rumbled, lusty and deep, and the pulse of need inside her grew exponentially.

His voice shook when he spoke. "Please tell me I can have more of that."

Dear God, he'd licked the fingers she'd used to masturbate.

He curled his fingers more deliberately around her wrist, locking her in place.

"Alex. What is wrong with—?"

Oh, sweet mercy.

He stared at her as he ran his tongue between her knuckles. Fire was in his eyes, his chest moving erratically as if breathing was difficult.

His eyes weren't human.

She was definitely talking to his bear, which meant something was happening, which meant...

Everything she'd heard over the years, plus all the research she'd done since discovering her mate was a polar bear, pointed to one thing. He was in mating fever, or about to be.

He is ours, her wolf said. *Pleeeaase.*

The whisper of information her friend Kaylee had shared slid in—the only way they could end up mated was if both of them agreed. And while Alex was here for some strange reason, and obviously wanting sex, that didn't mean he wanted her forever.

Which was what she truly wanted. What she truly *needed.* Instead, she was being offered temporary, and it was going to break her heart and hurt like hell, but turning him down? Impossible.

Lara laid her free hand against Alex's cheek, meeting his gaze head on. "Is it the fever?"

Happiness spread across his expression. He eased closer to press his body against hers. "Need you. But you choose—yes or no."

He shuddered, then shook his head violently in a move she recognized from having strongly worded arguments with her wild side. Obviously his bear did not agree with giving her the option of deciding.

There were so many good reasons to not do this, but having a chance to enjoy the big bad bear for a brief time outweighed everything.

"Are you sure you want me?" Lara asked softly.

An inhuman growl escaped his lips, and she found herself airborne. A second later, with Lara seated on the island, he pushed her legs apart and stepped against her. The thick ridge in his pants lined up perfectly with the aching softness between her legs.

Okay. Wrong question. "You physically want me, I got that, but are you sure you're not going to regret this later?"

He planted his hands on the island on either side of her. His head lowered and every muscle in his upper body bulged as he fought for control. When he lifted his head again, he was fully human, eyes full of questions and high intellect.

With his beast subdued, the man was ready to give an answer.

"You're smart and you're sexy. And you're a fucking ninja warrior woman, and if I'm going to experience mating fever with anyone, it's going to be someone who can kick my ass. I won't hurt you physically, I swear I won't, but I'm trusting you to have my back if the bear gets out of control."

Out of all the pretty promises he could've made, this was the only thing she couldn't resist. Offering his trust? It was one comment that set up something in her heart that really shouldn't be there—

Hope.

Lara pressed her hands to the sides of his face and leaned in. "Then I choose...*yes*."

11

_____

*H*e was still in control—the human him—but the bear was growing in strength. Alex wasn't sure how much longer he could stay at the reins, but hell if he wanted his first time with Lara to be a mindless rush.

Complications between them aside, there was no reason this had to be difficult. Hell, considering the inflammatory way they'd interacted before, he expected in the coming days they'd burn through a lot of calories and a whole lot of pleasure.

But right now, his partner for the next week was looking surprisingly frightened.

No. It wasn't fear in her eyes, but concern, and the sight of her wavering was enough to knock the bear back a notch or two.

Alex lifted a hand to stroke his knuckles over her cheek. "Thank you for your gift."

Her eyes widened.

He couldn't help it. A soft laugh escaped even as he slid his hand farther until he caught her nape. "Yes, I am capable of using pretty manners. Please, and thank you. And I have a few rules, such as a lady always goes first."

He leaned in closer, the scent of her body wrapping around them and making his skin twitch as if a million fireflies were brushing against him.

Hmmmm. Alex moved until his lips caressed hers then lowered his voice to breathe out the all-important question. "Speaking of which, did you come?"

Her breath hitched.

And that would be a no. Especially from the flash of blood rushing her cheeks, and didn't that kick his amusement up as well? She was shy in the bedroom.

Or the kitchen, as it were. Alex could work with that just fine.

"I think we'd better do something about me interrupting you."

"I have no objections, but can you give me a quick briefing on what to expect?" She ran her fingers through his hair, damn near petting him into submission. "I've never done this before."

He stilled. *Shit.*

Her cheeks quickly heated another couple of degrees, and she hurried to explain. "I've had sex before. I mean I've never been with— You have mating fever, and I don't know what that involves."

Valid question. "It means I'm going to take you a whole lot of times. Hard, soft, and everything in between. And not just fucking. I want to taste your body and tease you until you squirm. I look forward to stripping you naked and exploring you with my hands and my mouth and my cock until you're screaming my name. And your tits—oh, yeah, I plan to spend a lot of time on them. Bears like to play."

She wiggled slightly as he spoke but offered a head tilt

as if filing away information. "So, there's nothing I have to avoid?"

A beeper went off, the tone dragging over his nerves like nails on a chalkboard.

Lara swore and slipped out of his arms, heading across the room to pick up her phone and hit a button. Each step she took away from him felt as if knife tips sliced his skin.

She held up her phone, wiggling it in the air. "I've turned it off, but I have a massage booked right now."

An inexplicable rush of anger flared. Alex stomped to her side, catching her free hand in his. "Nobody touches you but me."

One of her brows rose slowly. "That would be rule number one. Gotcha."

As fast as it had flared, his anger faded. He lifted their joint hands between them. "I think we need to stay close. Being in contact with you calms me down."

"And that would be rule number two, but what do you mean *you think?* You've done this before."

He plucked the phone from her and laid it on the side table, stepping around her slowly. Keeping in constant contact as he trailed a hand up her arm and over her shoulder. Sliding his palm between her shoulder blades then lower. "I've had the mating fever before, yes, but I've avoided having access to any potential partners. This time is different."

She didn't need to know about the pact with his brothers or his grandfather's ultimatum.

Plus, it was time to stop talking. He stopped his slow stalking, standing behind her. Bodies nearly touching, he laid his hand over her belly on top of the softest cotton he'd ever felt. Then he leaned in close and brushed his cheek against hers. "Seems I owe you a massage."

She shivered but eased into him willingly. Pressing her head against his shoulder as he ghosted his lips down the side of her neck. "I spotted extra bottles of massage oil on the counter in the bathroom."

Alex had taken only half a step before an unzipping sensation shivered over his skin. Screw that.

He caught her under the knees and lifted her in his arms, snuggling her tightly as he strode through the enormous suite. "Nice digs, sugar."

"I won a getaway and got a free upgrade. In case you're wondering how I could afford this place, because I can't." She was stroking him again, fingers running through his short hair as if she was mesmerized.

He stopped beside a neat row of bottles filled with shimmering liquid and waited for her to scoop them up. He hadn't even considered how outrageously expensive the spa was since he'd seen the invitation—which was another thing he wasn't telling her about at the moment.

"Grab a towel," he ordered.

The instant she obeyed, he marched onward and through the massive arched entranceway into the next room.

The master bedroom was a work of art, with another fireplace and a wide window view overlooking the river. Center stage was a king-size bed with burgundy sheets and enough pillows to stage an epic battle.

It took a moment to organize everything the way he wanted it, and his bear thought he was out of his mind for not getting down to business, but when he finally curled a finger at Lara and motioned for her to come forward, the heavy-lidded expression in her eyes made it worthwhile.

Anticipation had clearly set up house in Lara, and every bit of her body quivered as he checked her over slowly.

Alex sat on the edge of the bed, knees wide, as Lara stood in front of him. "We're going to need to get rid of those pyjamas, sugar. Plus, we need to decide which massage oil we like best."

He handed her two of the "suitable for consumption" options, one for each hand, then twisted off the tops and put them aside.

Lara watched with amusement. "You make a mess and I'm giving you the cleaning bill," she warned.

"Then don't make a mess," he returned. "Your job is to keep those bottles steady."

"Piece of cake..." Her bold statement died off into a throaty moan as he caught hold of her pyjama top and slid his hands under it.

Palms pressed to the side of her body, he skimmed up her torso slowly. Slower still as his fingers teased her back. The higher his arms rose, the more the fabric bunched over her breasts. Lara raised her arms to the side, lower lip trembling. The heels of his hands brushed the outside swells of her breasts, and she whispered a soft curse.

"A massage is supposed to be *relaxing*, Borealis," she complained.

"We'll get there."

He stared at the naked skin he was slowly exposing— her belly, the dangling edge of the shirt teasing higher. Her nipples were taut peaks, the bottom edge of fabric catching briefly on them as their deep pink slowly came into sight.

He sped up, lifting the fabric and raising her arms along with it. Her fists were clenched around the bottles, but somehow even with her arms stretched over her head, she kept the liquid from spilling as he flipped the material off her wrists and tossed the top aside.

She breathed heavily, chest rising and falling, those

beautiful breasts on full display as she stood with her hands overhead.

His palms teased the soft skin of her forearms.

"Didn't spill a drop." Pride tinged her voice.

"Good for you. But we need a little spillage." Alex tightened his grip on her wrists. He changed the angle, tilting both bottles so the contents cascaded downward.

She gasped as oil splashed over her upper arms and torso. Rivulets of the heavy fluid pooled along her collarbone.

One line of liquid rolled over the top of her breast, coming to a stop at the very tip of her nipple. Moisture gathered until the perfect droplet formed.

His own modern art piece splayed with delectable finger paintable perfection.

Alex took the bottles from her hands and tossed them aside, holding her gaze as he exposed his hunger. "Now to decide which flavour I like best."

One finger. Just one, tracing the side of her neck and along the ridge of her collarbone. Following the line of wetness downward... downward...until he could swirl his fingertips in the oil and press his palm over her full breast.

A low rumble filled the room, and Alex smiled.

The sound came from Lara, her eyes closed, head falling back as he caressed her. He pressed her arms to her sides, skimming his palms over her limbs and rubbing in oil as he worked. His thighs supported her as she stood far enough away that he could tease and touch exactly the way he wanted.

And what he wanted was to work the oil into every inch of her skin. Her shoulders glistening, the pulse beating at the base of her neck shining with every pump of blood through her. Breasts smooth and silky against his palms, nipples dragging his skin with their sharp need.

He briefly covered her belly then swung his hands to her back, easing upward as he brought her even closer. Because the only thing that would make this better?

He stared at her tits while raw satisfaction swirled. "Taste test, sugar. Brace yourself."

Firm pressure between her shoulder blades brought her forward, and he wrapped his lips around her nipple.

12

------

*P*leasure rode her nerve endings hard enough Lara lost her breath.

What had been a teasing, almost silly moment with her standing half naked had taken a turn for the erotic so fast she still wasn't sure it was real.

But the drag of his mouth over her sensitive skin was real. The crisp jolt of pleasure as he slid his teeth over her nipple was real.

She was there, with him, and they were going to have sex, and she didn't know if she should laugh or cry.

Alex pushed at her pyjama pants, shoving them and her panties to the floor, and the next thing she knew, he'd lifted her. His back hit the mattress and her knees landed on either side of his shoulders. His hand braced her belly to help her catch her balance while his eyes, blazing with desire, stared up at her.

"I want to taste. I want to touch."

Before she could protest or ask for clarification—frankly before she could *think*—he'd slid down the mattress far enough that his mouth was in line with her hips.

At that point, any chance of using her brain was impossible. All that remained was sensation. His tongue slipping through her folds, circling her clit, stabbing as deep as he could go. He feasted as if he were a starving man, holding her tight against his eager mouth. No chance of escape—not that she was stupid enough to move.

Not when tension coiled harder inside her, dragging anticipation off the back burner and onto high heat. Simmering became a hard, rocking boil where her orgasm was the top blowing off the pan and the contents exploding all over the stove.

"Alex, oh, yes."

He was still staring, still driving her pleasure train, and she ground down on his face without thinking. Demanding every bit of satisfaction possible.

A rumble of amusement shook against her core in the brief second before Alex upped his game. And while she might have just come, that didn't matter to him as he assaulted her senses even harder, sending her reeling toward a second orgasm.

When she began to shake, body tightening around emptiness, the room whirled. She landed on her back, Alex rising over her as he rapidly stripped his clothes away. Desperation showed so clearly in his expression that she didn't have the heart to tease him.

It was a moment to be thankful for shifter genetics. No sexual diseases to worry about. And the other matter?

She laid her hands on his shoulders to get his attention. "I'm on birth control."

"Thank you," he breathed out in a rush. "I'm sorry. I just can't—"

He shook himself again as if trying to regain control, but Lara figured he only had so much of a leash on his inner beast. The fact he'd gotten her off twice already was a minor miracle.

From the grimace of pain on his face, he wasn't having a good time arguing with his bear.

Time for her to take control.

He wasn't expecting it, which was the only reason she got enough leverage in spite of his heavier weight pinning her. The slight give of the mattress helped as well, and the next moment he was under her and she was straddling him, rising on her knees and reaching down to take hold of his cock.

She stroked him. Once, then again. His eyes rolled back in his head and his jaw went slack.

"It's okay, sweetie," she teased. "You can show me more of your big bad bear moves later, but right now, I want this."

She tucked the broad head of his cock between her folds then slid down over him. Inch by delicious inch speared into her body and filled her to the brim.

Utter silence filled the room.

Lara's eyes were closed, and sometime in the last moment she'd forgotten to breathe. That had to be the reason why her head felt light and all her nerve endings were tingling. A lack of oxygen—it was the only logical explanation.

She dragged her eyes open and leaned forward, planting her palms on Alex's chest. His face was completely relaxed, the corners of his lips turned upward into the most self-satisfied smirk she'd ever seen.

"Don't you look like the cat that ate the canary," she teased.

Deep, dark pools of lust met her gaze as Alex ran his palms up her thighs to grasp her hips. "I'm the bear that ate the wolf. And I'm going to do it again later, but for now, this is pretty fantastic."

Tracing circles in the dark hair of his chest, Lara wiggled her hips the slightest bit. Just enough to savour the sensation of his thickness inside her. "You seem a lot calmer. Maybe we should stay like this for the rest of the week."

His expression darkened. "The hell we will."

She hadn't meant it as a challenge, but he seemed to have taken it as one. Which wasn't the worst thing in the world.

He curled toward her, abdominal muscles taut as he brought their torsos into contact. The oil on her skin slicked against him as he glided back and forth slowly, the hands on her hips moving her in the smallest of circles.

A personal massage of the most intimate kind.

He nipped at her lower lip. "Apologies for not bringing my A-game. Maybe we'll put in a rush order for this go-round, and I'll make it up to you the next dozen times."

Dozen times...

Sexy bear. Silly man for thinking two orgasms wasn't enough to already make her happy. Especially when she added in the parts she wasn't ready to tell him.

Like how being in his arms and having him look at her that way made something inside her soul very happy. Made her want to sink her teeth into him and never let go, even though she knew it wasn't time.

But the skin-to-skin contact was settling an ache she'd endured for the past six months, and as he kissed his way along her jaw to the sweet spot under her ear, Lara let herself enjoy every sensation to the fullest.

It was a lie, and it wasn't real, but it was sweet enough to ease the hurt for now.

But then his mouth made contact with her skin, teeth

rasping along her neck, and suddenly her wolf reared to the surface with a sharp inhale of anticipation.

Instinctively, Lara tightened her fingers in Alex's hair and jerked him back. Dear God, she didn't want to, but she had to make this clear.

She met his gaze straight on. "I like teeth, I won't lie, but don't bite my neck."

His bear stared back. Pondering, analyzing her words.

His eyes widened for a second. "Wolf secrets."

Pretty damn astute. She edged closer so he couldn't see her expression, instead kissing the corner of his mouth. "No biting," she repeated. "Now fuck me."

As if she'd opened the gates of a dam, Alex moved. His lips locked on hers and he kissed her frantically. Tongues tangling as he took control of her hips. Lifting slowly before bringing her down. Faster, harder.

His fingers pressed hard enough to leave bruises, but she didn't mind. Hell, she wanted it. Wanted it all. The heat rising between them, the building pressure in her core. The pounding demand on her sex as she used her thighs to help lift herself high enough so he could thrust upward without manipulating her body weight. Pulsating rhythm, a demanding assault on her senses.

His hands were free to roam and tease. Lifting her breasts high enough so he could take one nipple into his mouth then the other. Sucking and licking in a way that showed he was more than pleased to have her as a playmate.

When he slipped one hand between her thighs, thumb pressing over her clit, another wave broke. Her sex squeezed tight over his shaft as a cry burst from his lips.

He wrapped his arms around her and pulled her tight, burying his face against her neck so he could suck hard. Marking her in a primal way.

Heat in her core, heat wrapped around her from his torso, and the pulsating heat at her throat—

Almost perfect.

Alex slowly lay back on the mattress, legs still dangling off the bed, and Lara draped over him. He stroked his hands through her hair while their hearts pounded and their chests heaved, fighting for air.

Lara lay there and enjoyed every second. In spite of it not being real, it was delicious, and she would take every bit of him that she was offered.

She pressed her lips to his chest and offered a kiss before easing up far enough to look at his face. He was staring at the ceiling, hand still moving lazily through her hair.

"So?" Lara lifted a brow. "How was your dining experience?"

Alex smiled. "Not bad for an appetizer, but by the time we hit the main course in an hour or two, I think I'll have hit my stride."

Hysterical. She was about to make some comment about lofty dreams when she realized his cock was still inside her, and what's more, it was growing thick again.

His smile widened. He wiggled his hips and when a low gasp escaped her, his laugh rang out.

Alex cupped her face and kissed her, gently this time. "Remember. I did ask, and you did say yes."

Three hours later, Lara called mercy. He'd taken her a half dozen times, and in between he'd given her a massage, a foot rub, and more orgasms than she thought possible without irreversible damage.

She was on her front, fingers clenching the quilt as if that would stop her from puddling into a mass of goo and sliding off the bed. "Are you trying to fuck me to death?"

Alex flopped to the mattress beside her, legs tangled with hers. A sheen of sweat covered his brow, and his eyelids were at half-mast as he stared at her contentedly. "Breather? I could use a pizza or five."

Both their stomachs growled so loudly at that moment, the sound damn near echoed off the walls.

Lara laughed, blowing away a strand of hair that had fallen across her face because she didn't have the strength in her arms to move it with her fingers. "They have a Michelin-starred restaurant, and you're going to have pizza?"

"Oh, I'm going to have their signature dishes as well as pizza. You like pepperoni?"

"Vegetarian," she offered, just to watch him wince. "Kidding. Wolf, remember? Meat lovers. See if they'll offer a Bunny Special."

He snorted. "Damn. You remember that? That was a stroke of brilliance by whoever came up with the news article to cover up the fact the local Panago had a shifter-special topping option."

Lara willed her body into a sitting position, running a hand up his chest because she could. "Thank you, I was rather inspired that day."

Alex curled himself around her. "Seriously, that was you?"

"I had to do something. It was one of the damn Orion pack who sweet-talked the manager into adding bunny cutlets with spicy peppers and extra cheese to the menu. Security doesn't just mean keeping people out of places where they shouldn't be. It means spin-doctoring when necessary."

He made a face. "I don't think I would've had the

smarts to think of that one on the fly. My brother deals with that kind of bullshit. Good for you."

They crawled farther up the bed and leaned against the pillows as they examined the room service menu. They ordered an impossible amount of food then ducked into the shower.

Lara slapped his hands away a dozen times before she gave up, only escaping when the buzzer for the door went off.

Alex was still staring, hunger for more than food in his expression, as she tied on a robe and made her way to the door to let in the waitress.

Her name tag said Chantelle, and her mass of tight curls bounced as she strode forward pushing a cart layered with food. There was something about her that made Lara lean forward, curiosity growing as—

"I hope you find everything to your satisfaction." Chantelle glanced around the room before pulling an envelope from her pocket and handing it to Lara. The other woman spoke softly. "This is for you. Read it in private."

She left the room without another word as Lara stared at the envelope in her hand in horror.

Damn it, she'd thought she'd covered all the bases, and that this spa experience was on the up and up. Yet now she had an envelope in her hands that came from the pack office, and the woman who had just left had her sister's scent all over her—Chantelle had to have been at the pack house recently.

Something was wrong, and Lara had no idea how she was going to deal with it. Not without Alex discovering some secrets.

13

────────

*W*hile Alex had experienced the mating fever for years, as he'd shared with Lara, this was the first time he'd fully participated. His memory of avoiding the fever in the past had involved him shifting, and his bear was never great at remembering details.

This year was different on so many levels. Not only because he had a willing and, dare he say it, eager partner to play with, but his human side seemed to be doing a lot better at staying in charge.

Which sounded off the wall, but that was the problem with being both a man and an animal. They were the same person, and yet there were times his bear had a totally different sense of humour, among other things.

Thirty-six hours into the spa experience, and they hadn't left the suite even a single time. It hadn't been necessary, and for the first twenty-four, Alex been hard-pressed to move more than a few inches away from Lara. If he hadn't been inside her, he'd been touching her with as much of his body as possible.

Even when they'd had food delivered, he'd found it

hard to keep his hands off her. Lara had finally made the executive decision that they'd both stay locked in the bedroom while the waitstaff rolled masses of food into the living room.

Lara sat immediately beside him, legs tangled with his while she reached toward the coffee table to grab another serving of popcorn. The oversized robe she'd insisted on pulling on—in spite of his suggestion the suite stay a no-clothing zone—gaped open as she leaned back on the luxurious couch.

"You're out of control," she teased, motioning to the table with one hand. "I mean, I appreciate the calories, but five types of potato chips?"

She said she liked them, his bear insisted.

I believe you, he assured the animal, snorting with amusement because he didn't remember adding that portion to the last order they'd phoned in.

Yeah, bear-in-charge equaled weird shit on the menu.

Alex rearranged Lara on the couch beside him, pulling her feet onto the seat so her knees rose into the air. "Extra building supplies means it's playtime. Don't move."

He proceeded to grab a handful of chips from each bowl and arrange them on her body. Teeny towers of crunchy goodness bloomed on each of her knees and her shoulders.

When he leaned in to build a small Inuksuk statue on each of her breasts, Lara laughed softly. "You goof."

"No earthquakes allowed, sugar. Stay very, very still."

She waited motionless as he finished his task, the smile on her lips sincere and bright. "I didn't know you had a sense of humour like this."

Alex stared down at her as she good-naturedly put up with his inexplicable weirdness. A sudden jolt struck at the accuracy of her comment. "Bears like to play, but I haven't had a lot of chances lately."

Her expression softened. "It's tough when you're in security. It feels as if everybody expects you to be tough and ready at all times. And that's not a bad thing, but it's not the *only* thing. So I know what you mean. My wolf likes to play as well."

Alex ran a finger along her shin, the robe falling farther away to leave her legs bare to his teasing hands and drifting gaze. He touched as he spoke, wondering why his tongue was loosening. Why he was sharing this with her, but it felt right. It felt as if them being mostly naked meant their words needed to be naked as well.

Truthful and rawer than he'd admitted to anyone before. "My brothers are better at it than I am. At letting their animal sides be playful. Well, James is for sure. Cooper can get himself tied up in knots about doing things the right way, but even he has moments when he decides to shove the rules."

She could've been sitting in a Zen garden instead of covered with barbecue-chip dust and stacks of potato wedges. She seemed so serene and at peace.

Lara spoke carefully. "From what I know of your family, you've got a lot to be thankful for. If not getting playtime is something that needs to change, I bet they'd listen to you. They'd help you find a way for you to still be the security mastermind that you are but also get time off for the parts of you that need the break."

Alex eyed her closely. Despite how suspicious he'd been of her only days ago, his gut insisted this sharing time was completely aboveboard. As if she really was trying to make his world better.

"This is weird, isn't it? This whole you-and-me-sharing thing."

She met his gaze, and one brow rose high. "Are you kidding me? If potato chip body ornaments are a thing, then you and me chitchatting about feelings is situation normal."

He rumbled with amusement and moved toward her cautiously. "Body ornaments that are tasty. Let me check."

He managed to nibble one pile off her knee before he got distracted, and by the time they were done, the couch was covered in crushed chips and two sated bodies.

They fell into a routine. Sex, food, chatting. The sex was off the charts, the food fantastic, but by the evening of the second day Alex was beginning to look forward to the interludes where they ended up talking about anything and everything.

His bear good-naturedly rolled his eyes and seemed to be on his best behaviour, knocking almost politely to disrupt conversations when it was time for another round of heated sex.

Lara was sharing another story about being the youngest girl of five when there was a knock on the door of the suite.

She tensed, the happiness and relaxation in her body vanishing between one breath and the next.

Alex braced instinctively. "What's wrong?"

"Nothing." But her gaze darted to the door, shoulders tightening as if preparing to face an attack.

Warning signals going off, Alex rushed to the door. He glanced through the peephole and jerked the door open to find a startled waiter stepping back as he precariously balanced an oversized bowl in his hands.

"What?" Alex demanded.

The man's face had gone utterly white, but he held

forward his hands as if making an offering. "Delivery for Ms. Lazuli."

Alex let out a deep growl and took the container, watching as the man scampered away as if the hounds of hell were on his heels.

Weird.

He turned back and brought the delivery to Lara's side. "Did you order something?"

A frown folded her expression. She pulled a card from the top of the covering and opened it, and he read the message over her shoulder.

Sweets for the sweet.

She peeled back the edge of the lid and the scent of ripe blueberries filled the air. Nowhere near the dangerous item he'd expected from her earlier behavior.

Alex forced his voice into normal range, trying for light-hearted. "I hope you plan to share."

"Of course. Help yourself." She tipped the bowl toward him, but there was still tension in her shoulders. She was smiling, but it wasn't real.

Before he could ask any further questions, she picked a big ripe berry from the bowl and pressed it to his lips. One thing led to another, and the confusing situation slid from his brain as the mating fever once again took control.

Monday morning rolled around. Alex lay on the carpet in front of the fireplace with Lara sprawled on his back. She was tracing shapes with her fingertips on his shoulder blades, and he couldn't remember the last time he'd been so relaxed.

"This isn't done," he warned her. "I know we have to check out today, but I'm not out of the fever, so we need to talk about how we're going to deal."

She took a deep breath and let it out slowly, the air

gusting over his back as her cheek rested on his shoulder blade. "I can put off going back to the pack house for one more day, but beyond that, it could get tough."

He twisted, catching her as she fell and pulling her into his lap. The instant she'd spoken, the tension had risen so hard it was as if someone had been applying thumbscrews.

Alex gazed into her face, horrified to discover fear in her eyes. "Dammit. If being with me is going to cause trouble with your pack, I'll do what has to be done to smooth it out."

"It's not that," she hurried to assure him. "They have no control over who I choose to be with..."

The way her words faded off sent up all kinds of warning signals.

"Lara. What the hell is going on? You've been laughing and teasing and sharing with me for the past three days. Not just sex, but more than that, I can tell the thought of going back to the pack house is upsetting you."

Her expression grew even more guarded.

His bear went on alert.

Sudden clarity rushed in, and he was certain he knew what was going on. "Oh, hell. Your pack is up to something. What are they doing, Lara? What are they involved in that you can't bear to tell me?"

"Up to something? What are you talking about—oh *shit*." She hesitated.

Dammit. He lowered his tone and spoke as sincerely as he could. "At the risk of bringing up dangerous memories, I once told you friends were willing to help each other. I was trying to manipulate you back then, but now I mean it. Lara, I consider you my friend. You can tell me what's wrong, and I will help."

Brave and courageous wolf.

She looked him straight in the eye. "You want the truth?

Then here it is. Yes, I suspect my pack is up to no good, but that's not what's setting me off right now. The reason I don't want to go back is that my sister kindly sent a note to let me know she thinks it's time I find a partner. And since I didn't click with anyone in our local pack, she's invited a half dozen potential mates to come for a visit. The instant I go home there will be a horde of power-hungry wolves sniffing around to see if I want to hook up with any of them."

His bear shot past alert to nuclear fury.

Alex really wanted to respond to Lara, but at that moment he had to work on leashing the animal or who knew what would happen.

No leaving us, his bear demanded. *She's ours.*

I know. We're not done playing. Calm down and let me talk to her. Alex used a stranglehold on his animal side.

Wolf is mine, his bear screamed.

What followed wasn't easy to describe but mostly involved Alex fighting for control while his bear attempted to stomp around the room and shred things. Utter confusion, utter chaos.

Dangerous and deadly because most of him didn't give a damn who got hurt as long as Lara stayed safely by his side.

A firm grasp landed on his ear and hauled him to a stop. The connection grew from slight pressure to high-pitched pain, and then Lara was in front of him, her beautiful amber-flecked eyes glaring as if she were an avenging angel.

"You will stop this now," she said, power rolling out with the order.

A flash of fang and the sensation of claws had Alex's bear staring in rapt amazement. The wolfie power didn't really affect him other than by being hotter than hell, but the entire package of Lara laying down the law worked like a set of hand cuffs with an aphrodisiac chaser.

When he returned to his senses, he was sitting in the middle of the kitchen with killer wood. Lara straddled his hips, one hand knotted in the front of his shirt, the other running through his hair over and over in a move that had his inner beast purring like a kitten.

"I think I'm back," he informed her. He chose to ignore his aching hard-on, instead leaning forward to press his mouth to hers for a brief kiss. "Thank you."

One side of her lips curled upward, the twisted expression slightly amused and mostly sheepish. "Rule number three. Don't mention potential rivals without some warning. Trust me, Alex, I have zero interest in getting involved with any of the visiting wolves. But that's not important. We need to talk about how I help you finish dealing with the mating fever."

Screw that. At that point their problems were interconnected as far as he was concerned. "It's a simple solution. I figure we need at least four more days for me to be completely done with the fever. If you need to go home, then I'm coming with you."

Her jaw dropped. "I live at the pack house."

He offered a wide grin. "Then I guess this bear is moving in with the wolves."

14

————

The last fifteen minutes had been some of the weirdest of her entire life. Maybe she was dreaming. That would explain why Lara had just heard the impossible come out of Alex's mouth. "You want to move into the Orion pack house," she repeated.

His gaze drifted over her face and down her torso, fingers moving to the front of her robe to slowly untangle the knot she'd hurriedly put in position when she'd had to go ninja warrior on his bear.

"Yup. The pack house is adults-only, yes?" When she mindlessly nodded confirmation, a low growl rumbled up from his chest. "Perfect. I hope you have decent soundproofing between the bedrooms."

She snorted then covered her mouth with a hand. "Maybe I should request a room change. We can use the guest suite next to the common area."

Not that the soundproofing was any better there. But if she wanted to encourage the visiting wolves to leave her alone, the blatant sound of sex blasting from the room would be one way to ensure her unwanted guests knew she was currently occupied.

Alex slid his knuckle down her torso and over the swell of her breast, watching the progress of his hand intently even as he continued to speak. "Seriously, I mean it. I think we need to work together. I'll help you hold off the wolves, and we can figure out what mischief your pack is up to that's got both of our senses tingling. I'm right about that, aren't I?"

Lara struggled for a moment before admitting it. "You are, but I want you to promise to talk to me first if you find anything suspicious. I swear I don't want the pack doing anything rotten, but you can't go off half-cocked and bite off heads before we have a chance to let them make things right."

He nodded briskly. "From the stories you've told me about your sister, it sounds out of place for her to get involved in something truly hideous. We'll work together and figure this out."

She leaned her forehead against his. "Thank you. And thanks for helping me deal with the unwanted guests."

Annoyance shot across his face, but he kept his bear under control. "Believe me, I get how frustrating it is to have someone dictate matters involving your private life."

Inside, her wolf bumped against her, squirming with worry. *What if there's someone he's supposed to be with? Someone not us.*

Lara calmed her inner beast the best she could even as she scrambled for the strength to put words to her worry. "Someone out there demanding you get hitched?"

He laid his hands on her hips and made a face. "I told you this was my first official mating fever. I'd planned to avoid it this year as well, but due to some manipulation by my gramps, my brothers and I all agreed we'd let nature run its course." He held up a hand and placed a finger over her lips before she could ask a question. "Don't worry, you're not going to end up stuck with me. That was one good realization we had after James hooked up with Kaylee. Yes, my bear likes you, but there's no fear of us ending up mated without both our human sides agreeing we want to go all in."

Lara was speechless, her brain looping a million miles an hour. It was confirmation of what Kaylee had told her in passing, but to know that Alex had deliberately sought her out for sex knowing the end result would not be permanent—

The bit of hope that had been building over the past days snuffed out with a whimper.

It had been a fool's dream anyway, but they'd been getting along so well Lara had begun to hope that maybe there was a chance for more.

Alex had been honest and up-front the entire time. He'd said it was a one-shot deal, and she'd accepted that going in. And things *had* changed between them. They were no longer adversaries but were now working together. That part was good.

Inside, her wolf made a noise remarkably like a heart shredding in two. *Not enough. Friends is not enough. Want my mate.*

I know, baby. I know.

Then Lara pulled herself together because that's what she always did. She'd celebrate the relationship they'd built. The chance to be with him for the next few days was the crumb she would accept and enjoy with everything in her.

She dragged her palms against the scruff on his chin and focused on the bit gnawing at her that she could verbalize.

"If you plan to eviscerate your grandfather at any time, I'm available to help."

His laughter rang loud and clear through the luxurious suite. "He's a bastard, but we like him breathing. It's hard to hate the old man when he's positive he's being charming."

"Just saying, if you decide to get vengeance, I have your back."

Alex rubbed his nose alongside hers, his smile brightening the air around them with clear amusement. "Bloodthirsty vixen. I like that about you. I promise we'll work together, now with your pack, and down the road to give Gramps a hard time." He caught her wrist and slowly pulled her hand down his body, her palm sliding over ripped abdominal muscles and heading south. "Also, I promise nothing I do is ever *half*-cocked."

The thick length under her hand was perfect proof. "Proper protocol usually requires shaking hands on the deal."

Alex growled before pressing his fingers around hers in encouragement. "Let me help you with that."

FOUR HOURS LATER, THEIR COOPERATIVE INITIATIVE hit a snag.

After checking out, they had gotten into their own vehicles and driven back to Yellowknife. Lara had followed Alex back to his apartment where they took a short interlude to deal with the mating fever that had bloomed fiery hot during their brief time in separate vehicles. A.k.a. Alex pouncing on her the instant they got through the door. The heated session had left his living room furniture tipped over, an area rug bunched up under the dining room table, and a full body outline of her sweaty naked torso imprinted on the living room window.

Alex and the mating fever did not skip an opportunity. Lara was rather impressed.

Then they'd both shifted and gone exploring for a couple of hours. Her wolf had been delighted to move uninhibitedly through his territory. In his massive bear form, Alex had seemed utterly relaxed as they strolled beside the river and lazed in the afternoon sunshine. She'd curled up beside him and rested her chin on his paws, his warm breath rolling over her as he stared back at her.

Gentle. So very gentle as he playfully attempted to bat at her while she danced around him, far too agile to be caught.

It had been wonderful to play together as wolf and bear, and it eased a little of the pain still tearing at her heart.

Between the sex and the time in their animal forms, Lara had hoped it would be enough to keep him somewhat in control as she drove them to the pack house, and he seemed calm enough as she pulled into the parking space.

But by the time they got out of the car and she joined him on the sidewalk leading to the main entrance, Alex's eyes were fully bear.

It didn't help that a crowd had gathered on the front porch. Unfamiliar faces for the most part—and a rather handsome lot to be honest. But being confronted by six alpha male wolves didn't help Alex keep his temper in control.

Lara slipped her fingers into his, tugging to stop their forward motion. "How are you doing?" she asked quietly.

"Fantastic." The word was as close to a growl as could escape a human throat.

One of the reasons the pack house was located on the

outskirts of town was so random facts of shifter life weren't as obvious to the humans in town. Lara had many reasons to be thankful for that but never so much as now.

She turned to face Alex in the hopes of redirecting him to a different setting.

Too late. He'd already stripped off his shirt and was in the process of shoving his jeans and briefs off his lean hips. Boots were kicked free a second before he looked her in the eye...

And winked.

A moment later, a massive polar bear sat on the walkway beside her, a grin on his face and his head tilted to the side as if he were an innocent puppy.

Lara let out a long-suffering sigh then gathered up his clothes. "No bloodshed," she reminded him. Then she leaned down and touched her nose to his. "You are rather impressive. Also, did I mention how much cuter polar bears are than I expected?"

He narrowed his eyes, ears swiveling forward.

She grinned, ruffling the fur on the top of his head before stroking her fingers behind his ear to scratch softly. "I think we've lost some of our audience."

Alex rocked forward and head-butted her in the stomach, gentle but powerful enough that she had to scramble to keep her feet. She laughed and turned to the front porch to discover half of the unwelcome guests had vanished.

Unfortunately, that was the good news. The bad news was that her sister now stood front and center.

Crystal had her arms crossed over her chest and an unwelcoming expression on her face. "What the hell do you think you're doing?"

Lara stopped at the base of the stairs, body on alert. At

least until Alex rumbled up beside her, one paw on either side of her legs, surrounding her.

She got the message—he had her back.

She lifted her chin and met her sister's gaze. "You commanded me to return to the pack house, so I'm here. Unfortunately, I was in the middle of something I can't call off."

Crystal rolled her eyes. "Please. You're fucking him—I can smell it from here. Do it on your own time and somewhere else."

"Can't. Mating fever."

Her sister's frown deepened. "Get out. He's not mated to you. I can tell."

Pain shot through Lara at the comment. It was true—they might be fated to be mates, but they weren't actually mated at the moment.

Lara pulled on sarcasm like armour. "Nope. But for whatever reason, possibly because of a certain little 'make friends and influence people' situation you put me in earlier, Alex and I *are* involved for the duration. It's a bear thing. It's not our way, and it doesn't make sense to you, but it's something we have to respect."

Slow curses rumbled from Crystal's lips before she shook her head and stormed into the pack house, leaving the door open behind her. A final shout rang over her shoulder. "If he breaks anything, he's paying for it."

Lara stepped forward, meeting the gaze of each wolf who had been summoned by her sister. Only two of them managed to hold her gaze for any length of time.

The one who dared take a step closer tumbled off the porch a second later. Alex, seemingly by accident, had swung a massive hip, making contact with the man's thighs and sending him flying.

Lara laughed. She placed a hand on Alex's furry shoulder and led him into the pack house. As a homecoming, it was the weirdest ever, yet she wouldn't have changed a thing.

Well, maybe one thing. When she got him alone in her quarters, she needed to sweet-talk the bear into changing back to human.

She leaned in close and murmured in his ear. "Did I mention you getting all growly gets me hot?"

She should've waited. A second later a very naked, very riled up Alex was stalking her deeper into the pack house. "You've got thirty seconds to find a private place, or I won't be held responsible for what's definitely not going to be a PG event."

Lara set off at a run, Alex pounding after her. She made it to her room in seventeen seconds, had the door closed behind him at twenty-four, and her clothes off by twenty-nine.

Challenge met.

Alex stared her down as he stepped closer, catching her fingers in his and bringing their bodies into contact. "Wolf hearing is really sensitive, isn't it?"

Oh shit. She pinned her lips together, heart rate increasing at the expression in his eyes.

His grin widened. "By the time I'm done tonight, I'll make you scream my name so many times everyone in the Orion pack house will be looking for earplugs or moving to the Motel Six for some peace and quiet."

He did.

And she did.

It was pretty certain that they did as well.

15

___

*T*he next four days were a blur.

Alex had some vivid memories, especially of the killer sex and his and Lara's ongoing conversations, but between those highlights there were a lot of things that didn't seem real.

Like the way his bear refused to cooperate and behave politely in the pack house. Alex had been taught from the time he was very young that shifting was natural and getting naked in preparation for a shift was acceptable but not something you prolonged or flaunted.

And yet he caught himself more than once striding through the pack house buck naked, pausing at the edges of conversations. He might've spent a little time flexing his muscles during these excursions.

It wasn't his fault that polar bears tended to be a couple sizes larger than your average wolf, whether in animal or human form. And surprisingly, after a few of these impromptu visits, the number of wolves brought in for Lara's perusal seemed to have diminished.

He also shifted to his polar bear and made his way

downstairs to sit in the middle of the common area, glaring at the most annoying of the wolves until Crystal, shaking her head, led him back to Lara's apartment.

The Orion pack Alpha pointed firmly into the room.

Alex obligingly sauntered in, rubbing his big head along Lara's bare leg—the one that was sticking out from under the covers from where she'd collapsed face down after their last session. He'd left her rather exhausted.

Smug satisfaction welled at that thought.

He crawled onto the mattress at her side.

She rolled and tangled her fingers in the fur by his ears. "Alex?"

"Keep your pet under control," Crystal growled from her position at the door.

Lara twisted to face her sister, blinking away her sleepiness. "What?"

"He's a menace. Keep track of him—he was wandering the pack house again."

"I swear I just fell asleep for a minute. I don't know why he took off."

Crystal huffed. "Then stop sleeping. You need to keep a better eye on him. I don't care if it is *the bear way*, he's not allowed to play handball with our pack mates."

Lara seemed confused. "We...don't have a handball court."

"I know." Crystal sniffed in Alex's direction. "He used a pack mate as the ball and the wall of the garage as his court."

Lara kept still until Crystal slammed the door shut after herself, and then she laughed as she pushed to her knees and wrapped her arms around his neck, completely comfortable with his furry self.

Of course she's comfortable. What's not to love? his bear gloated.

Alex took control and shifted back to human even as he chuckled inside. *No problem with your ego.*

Also in the category of strange were the weird presents that kept arriving for Lara. On Monday, it was a set of ninja movies. Tuesday, a huge bouquet of tulips arrived—God knows where they had been brought in from in September.

But the most...*aromatic*...was the morning they opened the door to discover a children's swimming pool filled with fish in the middle of the hallway.

The fact it was fresh-caught trout and enough to feed the entire pack soothed over the wolves who were still eyeing Lara with confusion for bringing Alex home without much explanation.

Interestingly, his bear didn't seem put out at all by the gifts.

"They're far more charming presents than I expected from tone-deaf suitors," she said, sniffing the air as the scent of chocolate truffles filtered across the room from the enormous box lying open on the mantle. "It has to be someone trying to make a good impression."

"Is it working?" he asked.

She arched a brow, staring at him intently. She lay naked on her back under him, chest still heaving from their most recent bout of sex. "Oh, definitely. Haven't you seen me running up and down the halls of the pack house looking for someone to fool around with because it's been simply *ages* since I got any."

Alex offered a wicked grin. It felt good to be able to tease her and watch her heart kick up a notch as the pulse pounded at the base of her throat. "If you've still got energy to burn, then I guess I don't have to wait to do *this*..."

Iᴛ ᴛᴏᴏᴋ ᴀ ꜰᴜʟʟ ᴡᴇᴇᴋ ʙᴇꜰᴏʀᴇ Aʟᴇx ꜰᴇʟᴛ ᴄᴏɴꜰɪᴅᴇɴᴛ enough that the fever had passed and they could venture out into public.

The week together had been interesting. Alex was gratified to know he'd made it through another year unscathed. No mate bond had appeared, although he had a new appreciation for the woman who'd helped him.

His regard wasn't only sexual, although he'd be willing to go for a repeat anytime she offered. Somewhere in the past week, Alex had gotten to know Lara better. The stories they'd shared and the honest conversations meant she was now three-dimensional. She was no longer an unknown enemy but someone trying her best, same as him.

Laughter bloomed beside him, and Alex glanced up to discover his brother Cooper shaking his head in amusement.

Cooper turned to Lara, who sat beside Alex at the oversized table. "Are you sure he's done with the fever?"

"Why are you asking her?" Alex demanded. "I'm right here."

James was across the table with his arm curled around his mate. "Because you're here in body, but a moment ago you were totally distracted, staring into space."

The brunette sitting beside him tilted her head then grinned. "It's just not like you, Alex. You're always so intense and focused. Especially considering where we are."

Kaylee gestured around them.

She was right. Considering they were gathered at a large table at Sirius Trouble, the wolf-run roadhouse, Alex should've been a lot more on edge.

Especially considering he and his brothers rarely dropped in at the competition. Plus, there were women with them—Kaylee for one—and Amber, the head secretary from Borealis Gems.

Plus Lara, of course, but at least her being there made some sort of sense.

Her presence was probably why he wasn't bothering to pay attention. There'd been a brief pause when he and Lara had marched through the doors, but after a week of seeing Alex invade the pack house, conversations went back to normal pretty quick.

Then his brothers had shown up.

Yet all it'd taken for the wolves to settle down was for Lara to walk across the room and welcome them. There were still murmurs, but they were few and far between, stifled as soon as Lara glanced at the offending pack mate and sent out a shot of wolfie mojo.

"No need for me to be on high alert when she's got it under control." Alex grinned at Lara. "Seems you said something about having better food here than we have at Diamond Tavern. Put up or shut up," he ordered.

They'd taken the largest table possible, and while the food arrived in waves, conversation moved briskly.

"What's your plan now that the fever's over?" Cooper asked.

Lara and Alex exchanged glances before he answered quietly. "I'm staying at the pack house for a bit. We're working on a project together."

Amber's eyes grew wide. She hauled a pad of paper out of her purse and quickly scribbled a note, sliding it across the table to Lara.

Does this have something to do with that thing we discussed a while ago?

Alex kicked himself. Of course. That's why Lara had been hanging out with Kaylee and Amber. Not to try and cause trouble, but to help solve it. He should've assumed the women would be a step ahead of him on this.

Lara jotted a quick answer and pushed it back, which was a really smart thing considering the power of wolf hearing. Even a whispered conversation about this would spread like wildfire.

Yes. We're looking into it. I'll let you know ASAP.

Lara made no mention of her potential-partner-alpha-wolf issue, but there was only one straggler still hanging on, and the longer Alex was around, the weaker his interest seemed.

Not the way Alex would've done it if he was intent on a woman. If the dudes were so easily discouraged, they obviously didn't deserve someone like Lara.

The conversation rotated to topics that were a little more neutral.

"How goes the search for your brother?" Alex asked Amber. It was the reason the woman had moved to the north in the first place a couple of years ago—tracking down her only sibling.

She made a face, staring forlornly at the french fry in her fingers. "The last lead faded to nothing. I know he's here somewhere, but there are so many small communities over the territory that don't keep in touch on a regular basis. It's hard to know what to do next."

"Won't you let me check with the wolf hotline?" Lara offered. "We've always got members taking time off and running wild. They get to just about every village and settlement over the course of the winter."

Amber glanced at Alex, hopefulness rising in her eyes. "I think—"

Damn. He wondered if his animosity toward Lara earlier in the year had made Amber hesitate to accept the help before this.

No, he hadn't trusted Lara. Before. But while wolves still made him uncomfortable and there was something big looming, in regard to *this*, if she said it might help, she meant it.

He inclined his head in a private message of approval for Amber.

Her eyes lit up and her smile grew wide. She nodded firmly at her friend. "I would appreciate it. I can get you all his details when we're home tonight."

Lara nodded then raised a hand momentarily and excused herself from the table. "Sorry, guys. I need to deal with this."

She made her way to the other side of the room where a pair of wolves were glaring intently at each other. Lara folded her arms over her chest and leaned her head to one side, listening to one comment then the other before speaking quietly in return.

Alex watched as the tension drained away and the two men shook hands instead of flailing fists at each other the way he would've expected from their earlier stances.

It took Lara nearly twenty minutes to get back to the table, not just because she dealt with trouble before it could brew, but because the wolves genuinely seem to like her and wanted to talk.

It made no sense at all, but that realization made something inside Alex feel almost...proud. She spoke with people at many of the tables, nodding reassuringly as a few worried glances were tossed toward the bears.

A laugh drifted from her, and their eyes met. She winked, and his sense of amusement grew. As if she was saying it was okay for him to be there in her territory, and what's more, she liked him there.

Somebody put *Teddy Bears' Picnic* on the sound system.

Lara was still watching, the corners of her lips twisted upward as she rolled her eyes momentarily and shrugged her shoulders as if to say it was just wolf hijinks.

Alex leaned forward and interrupted the conversation. "Excuse us, ladies, but I need my brothers to join me for a few moments."

James kissed Kaylee briefly before sliding out from the table. Cooper eyed Alex curiously, but also stepped forward.

Amber nonchalantly waved a hand in the air, but her eyes widened and her cheeks heated when Alex stripped off his clothes then stacked them neatly on the chair beside her.

James snorted in amusement, but a moment later he was also naked.

Cooper pinched the bridge of his nose, grimacing as he stepped behind Kaylee's chair, stripped and shifted so quickly he nearly got tangled in his clothing.

Across the room, Lara was outright laughing as Alex turned and offered a salute before joining his brothers in bear form.

The wolves cleared room for him as Alex sauntered forward, meeting Lara on the middle of the dance floor.

"You're such a goof," she declared, laughing even harder as he made his way to his hind feet and held out his hands as if waiting to waltz. "No way, sweetheart. All it takes is for you to make one wrong move and I'd end up a pancake."

But when he went back to four paws, Lara wrapped her

arms around his head, dancing on the spot as he shuffled his front paws back and forth. To their right, Kaylee laughed wholeheartedly as James sat on the hardwood and swung his paws in time with the music.

Cooper? He was motionless as Amber stood at his side. The little human was shaking in her boots, but remained protectively alert as if ready to wallop anyone who got too close. Which was really funny considering that when Cooper was in bear form, a single paw was nearly the size of her head. One small swing would send any attacker flying.

Something amazing and happy swirled into Alex's heart. In that brief moment, he wasn't the security expert and defender of his family—he was simply Alex. Having fun and relaxing with friends and family.

Yet even as they played in this wholly unexpected way, Alex still knew exactly what was going on and where the danger points were. And the ones he couldn't see, like the door at his back, Lara was facing. She had it under control.

The music changed. *Let Me Be Your Teddy Bear* rang out, and a howl of laughter went up from all the wolves present. Some of them shifted to fur and crowded onto the floor to join the party.

The dance went on.

16

$\mathcal{L}$ara was curled up in the oversized rocking chair at the edge of the common room. She had a book in her lap, fingers tucked between the pages because she'd reread the same paragraph over and over for the last half hour.

Fall had officially arrived, and it was cool enough to have a fire burning in the fireplace. A couple dozen pack members were gathered around the room enjoying the quiet evening.

Alex was somewhere wandering, which in itself was decidedly fascinating to think about. Even though he could've left a week ago, he'd stayed until the final visitor Crystal had invited gave up, good-naturedly offering Alex a pat on the back and not even attempting to get close enough to Lara to shake her hand in farewell.

Since that time, Alex remained, and while every morning she braced herself for his announcement that he had to get on with his life and go do the next thing, she was more optimistic that sometime in the future she'd be able to approach him about broadening their relationship.

Her wolf had given up speaking to her, disgusted that they weren't simply coming out and laying their cards on the table.

But she wouldn't do that to him. The incredibly intimate contact they'd had over the past two weeks meant she'd grown to appreciate Alex's sincerity. When he gave his word, he gave it one hundred percent. She could trust him, and that was good, but that meant he had to be able to trust her as well.

They'd gone into this saying there would be no expectations and no fallout, and no matter how much it hurt, she was going to stick to that agreement.

Maybe she'd give him a month or two to explore the friendship thing, but then she was going to revisit the idea of a real relationship, and she was going to be tenacious about what she wanted—but not now. It wouldn't be right.

Her senses tingled five seconds before Alex walked through the door, as if she was still sensitized to his approach. He motioned farewell to the couple of guys he'd been talking to then turned unerringly toward her and stalked his way across the room.

Lara smiled up at him. "Did you get lost?"

She gasped as he lifted her, twisting smoothly and settling in the chair with her delicately balanced in his lap. "Nope. I knew exactly where I was at every moment."

A chuckle rumbled from Alex. How had she thought he was stiff and unyielding?

Although, she'd always known he was sexy beyond belief, and as he tipped her chin and pressed his lips to hers, she ignored everything except savouring the moment.

A thump sounded—her book hitting the floor, but her fingers were in his hair and he was easing her against him as he leaned back in the rocker and his tongue danced with hers, sending her senses reeling.

"Get a room," someone shouted, but beyond snickers of amusement, there was nothing but acceptance from the gathered crowd.

Lara pulled back to meet his amused gaze. "You're ruining my reputation."

"I don't see how. Kissing in the common room doesn't affect your status as the most kick-ass warrior in the room." His gaze fell to her lips. "But maybe we should try again, just to be certain."

Resistance was futile. She leaned into him harder and kissed him back enthusiastically, mentally debating how soon she could haul him out of the chair and actually follow that directive to go to their room for more than kissing.

Alex was the one to pull back the next time, speaking soft enough that with the music playing overhead it would take concentrated effort for even the wolves in the room to hear him. "I found something."

For a moment, his words didn't register. Then as she began to stiffen, he ran a hand down her back and raised a brow in warning.

Oh my God, he'd been snooping somewhere in the pack house and had actually found some information. "Proof?"

He wrinkled his nose. "Something that needs your signature. No data, just those pages, so it says something is going on but not *what*."

The relaxation she'd felt moments earlier was gone as a sense of destiny struck. It was good that he'd found something because this needed to be solved before anything else could happen, but damn if she didn't want to go back to the days of lying in bed with him with no agenda except making each other happy.

Except, this also made her happy. Solving the puzzle and getting to find a solution meant an end to being in limbo.

She straightened carefully. "Then this is happening. I need to take action."

"Now don't go off half-cocked," he warned. "Talk to your sister. Ask her what's going on and give her a chance to make it right."

Lara felt something inside her twist with amusement and a deep sense of rightness at hearing his suggestion. "Awesome. You're feeding me back my own words."

"They were pretty smart to begin with," he admitted sheepishly. "I figured why try and improve on perfection?"

He took a deep breath, placing a hand over her heart. Steadying her as she gathered her courage.

"I can do this," she whispered. "It's right that I do this."

"You can do anything," he agreed.

He kissed her fiercely, none of the playfulness that had been there earlier remaining. It was intense and powerful, and as much of a promise as any she'd received.

When she crawled off his lap and straightened her shoulders, he uncurled himself and stood at her side, waiting patiently.

Lara marched across the room to where her sister sat behind a massive oak CEO's desk. Unlike the working one in the office, this one was all about intimidation and presence. It didn't matter that Crystal was currently working on a jigsaw puzzle on the surface, the space screamed *I am the one in charge, don't interrupt me.*

Lara stopped in front of the desk, legs set wide, fists resting on her hips. "Crystal."

Her sister waved a hand as if shooing away a fly. "I'm busy."

Lara leaned forward, placing her hand on top of the open space left in the puzzle and blocking Crystal's work. "I heard something that's got me worried, and I'd like to talk about it. Would you mind if we go somewhere private?"

A rude snort shot from her sister. Crystal leaned back in her chair and looked Lara up and down with barely a glance to the side at Alex. "Oh, honey. You want some privacy? Oops, sorry. That's not the wolf way. You got something to say, you say it right here in front of everyone."

It didn't feel right. Lara glanced at Alex then back at Crystal. The words were taunting, as if she were trying to cause a fight. "Why are you doing this?" Lara muttered softly.

Crystal shot to her feet. "Because I'm a wolf. And because I'm the Alpha, and because it's what needs to happen. What's *your* problem?"

Lara had tried. She'd really tried, but it seemed her only option was to go straight through her sister.

She took a deep breath. "My problem is you're up to something. Possibly something illegal, or at least that's my suspicion. But I hope to hell you aren't. That you're not dragging the Orion pack into something that's going to tear us apart. So, since we're doing this the wolf way, how about you relieve my suspicions right now and explain why there's paperwork that requires my signature for some sort of deal that I don't even know is going down?"

"Not very trusting, are you?" Crystal snapped.

They had the attention of every wolf in the room, with more trickling in through the open doors. Power leaked from Crystal, but Lara was more than able to stand up against it.

Anger and frustration gave her the ability to speak power for power. "I refuse to let this pack be involved in any criminal activity. I choose to make the right decision for our future."

"But you're not the one in charge, are you?" Crystal stepped from behind the desk. "I've been more than patient with you recently. I think it's time for you to be quiet and go sit in the corner. Take your Pooh Bear with you—he's the perfect stuffed animal to keep the little girl company."

Did her sister really think a few insults were going to make her lose her temper? This was about so many things that were much more important.

And while Alex had plenty of reasons to be pissed, he was keeping his temper amazingly well. In fact, as she met his gaze, there was approval there. Encouragement even. He folded his arms across his chest and glared at Crystal.

All the events of the past six months bundled together, momentum building until it led to this moment. Lara had to decide if she was ready.

There really was no other choice.

She lifted her chin and met Crystal's gaze square on. "I'm not letting you do this, sis..."

"Are you going to stop me?"

"Yes."

The few murmured voices in the background flared briefly before settling again, every eye in the room fixed on them as power swelled.

"So you're challenging me. I wondered if this day would ever come." Crystal glanced over her shoulder, and out of nowhere, Auntie Amethyst marched to her side. Her purplish platinum hair was done up in a fancy do, the frames of her glasses an exact match. Her neat golf shirt looked fairly formal until you realized the logo was of two wolves in an indelicate position.

Together, the two of them marched to the centre of the room, face to face with Lara.

Heart pounding, Lara adjusted her footing a little more firmly. This had to be done, and it was the right thing to do. Didn't mean she had to like it.

She tried one final time. "We don't have to do this. You can make a different choice."

"But I like this choice right here," Crystal said softly, never taking her eyes off Lara. "Name your second so we can get started."

The silence that had been in place for the past few moments shattered, the entire pack raising their voice as Alex stepped forward and linked their fingers together.

17

Alex had no idea wolves could make such horrific noises.

Lara squeezed his fingers then let go, squaring her shoulders as she faced her sister and prepared to fight.

Annoyance painted Crystal's features as she glanced in Alex's direction dismissively. "He's a bear. Pick someone else."

The order snapped out with the force of a command, yet the woman at his side shrugged easily as if she weren't face-to-face with the most powerful wolf in the room.

"There's nothing in the rules that says I can't have someone other than a wolf at my back. I choose him. I *want* him."

The rush of sheer pleasure shooting through Alex's veins would've been more enjoyable if it hadn't been for the potential bloodshed. It was as if Lara's words tied them together tighter, an invisible bond declaring what they'd discovered over the past weeks. They were good together, and in this case, he was ready to stand at her side.

The Alpha of the Orion pack turned her glare on him.

"You can't offer to be her second. It's outrageous, and besides, you have no idea what you're promising. It's a *wolf* thing."

Annoyance broke through the pulse beating between him and Lara. He glared at Crystal. Number one, no one was telling him what he could and couldn't do.

Number two, that was bullshit.

He spoke loud and clear, his words cutting through the din created by the pack members. "Maybe I don't know all your customs, but I believe in Lara. I believe her when she says she wants nothing but the best for the pack, and that includes wanting the best for you. If you were any kind of sister, you'd listen, because she loves you a hell of a lot. But no matter what happens next, I'm ready to stand with her. To support her, and fight at her side, and if it means mourning with her because you're no longer around, so be it."

Seemingly unimpressed, Crystal rolled her eyes. "And they say wolves are bloodthirsty." She grinned, teeth showing. "You mean you're going to step in and fight for her?"

"She doesn't need me to. She can fight her own battles because she's strong and smart, but she's got all the backup she needs."

It took everything in him to stand down. Remaining alert, Alex adjusted his feet until he stood far enough back so he was no longer guarding the woman he loved—

For fuck's sake. He loved her.

Told you so, his bear murmured happily.

Yeah, yeah, gloat later. We're a little busy right now.

Five paces in front of him, Auntie Amethyst mirrored his actions, stepping to one side to leave Lara and Crystal on their own. Close enough that she could undoubtedly shoot across the space to confront him or anyone else who chose to interfere.

He glared at her, angry she was willing to allow the sisters—

Auntie Amethyst winked.

Slow and deliberate, accompanied by a snap of her gum that made him jerk back in confusion. Displaying zero tension in her body, the older woman folded her arms then turned her attention to the challenge in the middle of the room.

Was it a message of some kind, or a double cross? The timing made it suspicious.

Only, from the stories that Lara had shared, she liked her auntie—other than the woman's nicotine habit. The fact Amethyst didn't let anyone get away with bullshit had been something Lara admired.

Power surged around him, and his attention swung back to Lara. He used his peripheral vision to maintain watch on the rest of the pack, but his gaze was locked forward.

There was a whole lot of woo-woo stuff happening, and none of it in the physical realm.

While Alex acknowledged there had to be magic involved in being a shifter, outside of the human-to-animal change, polar bears pretty much followed human traditions to figure out their hierarchies. Occasionally the person to win a fight was the one who could sit on the others for the longest, which might mean physical strength, but just as often it involved being mentally wily like his gramps.

But with wolves? Physical strength was part of it, but the crazy dominance power was a hell of a lot more important, and right now Alex was getting a front-row seat to observe exactly what that meant.

Crystal and Lara were face to face, staring each other

down. Power radiated from both of them, charging the air with energy as if an electrical storm were contained in the room. The bossiness didn't really affect him too much, but as the rumble in the room ebbed and flowed, it was obvious the rest of the pack mates knew exactly who was winning at any particular moment.

Lara's power tasted different than her sister's. Crystal's felt sharp and almost smoky, but as Lara leaned forward, pushing against an invisible force, sweet citrus rolled over the air. Another brilliant, refreshing burst struck, and Crystal winced.

Ready for anything, Alex waited in case he needed to shift and stop anyone from interfering. But it seemed this battle was not going to be decided by fangs and fur, but instead entirely by this invisible presentation of Lara's indomitable will.

Because it was clear she was winning. Not just in how she stood straighter, strong and determined, but how the pack began to murmur her name. Chins dipping and eyes brightening.

Crystal staggered back a half step, flinching as if in pain.

Lara hesitated, and the sheer volume of energy in the room eased back slightly. Alex wanted to warn her to be careful, to make sure she wasn't leaving herself vulnerable.

She's got this, his bear assured him. *Wolf is being kind.*

As long as she doesn't get hurt, he told the beast.

Our wolf is brave and smart.

Alex wasn't about to argue. Not when the proof was right there in front of him.

She held a hand out to one side as if to warn him not to act, then she swung her hand toward her sister. Power flared briefly, filling every available space in the room.

Lara straightened to her full height. Crystal cringed, and...something changed.

The prickly, electric flavour on the air changed to one of soothing. Soft and caring, as if everyone were being wrapped in a warm, protective blanket.

Around the room, wolves collapsed onto sofas and relaxed on the floor, something close to puppy adoration crossing their faces as they stared at Lara, although Alex wasn't sure he wanted to point that out to them.

Crystal still stood, but her chin drooped and her muscles quivered as if she'd run a marathon.

One second. Another, then Lara stepped forward and caught her sister's hand. "Yield."

Crystal took a deep breath, and for one horrible moment, Alex thought she was about to gather everything she had and attack one last time.

What she did was throw her arms around her sister, tears streaming down her face as she gasped, "They're yours. I yield. Thank you."

Embracing her hard, Lara patted her sister on the back, twisting so she could face Alex. A crease between her brows, she mouthed the words at him. *Thank you?*

Alex shrugged. There didn't seem to be a good explanation. And there was a lot of action in the room that was distracting him.

Wolves were coming forward both to hug Crystal and to offer Lara their allegiance. Most the time that involved a firm handshake, but also the occasional hug and a few kisses on the cheek.

Alex wasn't sure what he thought about those, but this was one time his bear was willing to withhold judgment in case it was a wolf thing.

"Don't worry. They're claiming her in a totally different way than you have in mind."

Auntie Amethyst stood in front of him, the scent of smoke rising from her powerfully enough to make his eyes water.

He managed to keep from coughing, but his voice was still lower than usual. "Have you considered trying the patch, and what are you talking about?"

She tilted her head toward the chaos only a few feet away. "Lara's the new Alpha. She belongs to us, and we belong to her, but I think she's still got room for you. Just don't drag it out. It's always better to get these things resolved in an orderly fashion."

He eyed the woman and wondered if it would be rude to take a bite out of her. "How on earth is that any of your business?"

Lara's aunt made a face. "Interesting..."

A snort escaped before he could help it. "I've heard that's the phrase you use when you have *opinions*."

She looked delighted. "So, you have been talking as well as screwing. That will help a lot going forward." She leaned toward him slightly. He leaned back in order to not get drowned by the scent of smoke. "Trust me, we've kinda had this planned for a while. Once the dust settles, you'll understand everything."

Which would be a good thing because right then, the only thing he understood for sure was that Lara was reaching the end of her meet-and-greet, and he wanted to be at her side.

Okay, he also knew he wanted to find somewhere private so he could assure himself she was one hundred percent okay with what had just happened.

He also wanted to strip off her clothes and do wicked,

dirty things to her because, holy hell, that display of power had been hot.

Hmmm. It seemed he had *quite* a to-do list, and he'd like to get started on it as soon as possible.

"Maybe we should finish this later," he suggested to Auntie Amethyst.

"No problem. One thing... You should know I don't take advice from random strangers. But if you do things the right way, and we actually end up related, then I might consider looking into that patch thing." She waved a hand in the air. "Everybody back up and give us some space. We got shit to do, so you all get started on what needs to be done."

Wolves scrambled to get out of the way, vanishing down hallways as the old woman marched Crystal, Lara, and Alex into the pack office.

"Sit," Auntie Amethyst ordered Lara, pointing at the chair behind the desk.

Lara arched a brow. "So much for the concept that nobody bosses the Alpha around."

"Pshaw. I ain't bossing you around. Just taking care of the details."

She grabbed a folder off the top of the filing cabinet and spread a dozen pieces of paper on the desk in front of Lara.

Lara glanced at them, jaw slowly dropping. She met Alex's gaze before turning to her sister. "Transfer-of-power papers. These are for the pack?"

Crystal was still trembling as if being slammed with power had drained the energy right out of her, but her grin was sheer mischief. "Humans don't accept the explanation 'her wolf is more powerful than mine' when it comes to accessing bank accounts. All of this gives you legal control of the pack and everything related to Midnight Inc. that I used to control."

Understanding was slowly rising. "You've had this planned for a long time," Alex said, glancing at Lara's sister.

Crystal nodded, still obviously proud of herself even as she collapsed into a chair. "Sorry. My legs don't want to hold me right now." She looked across at Lara, pride in her expression. "I knew you were strong enough to take over, and after fifteen years of leading the pack, I'm ready to do something different. But if I'd tried simply abdicating, you would've had a dozen or more challengers—that's what happened to me when Mom and Dad handed over control. You were probably too little to remember what a pain in the ass it was, but I didn't see why you should have to put up with that bullshit. I know you could beat them, but somebody might have gotten hurt."

"Doing it the sneaky way meant less chance of bloodshed…" Lara nodded slowly. "That explains some of the things I overheard. Some of the rumours that got out are what set Alex tracking down information about hostile takeovers."

A swear escaped Crystal, and she snapped her head to the side to stare aghast at Alex. "Oh my God, did you think we were trying to do something to Borealis Gems? No. Not at all. I would never dream of doing anything to hurt my sister's ma—"

She went off into a coughing fit the same instant Lara did.

Auntie Amethyst rolled her eyes and slammed down bottles of water in front of the two women. "Ladies, if you could hold yourself together for another few minutes, Alex and I need to witness whatever needs to be signed."

It took a few minutes to pass around the pens, but in the end, a stack of papers was lined up on the edge of the desk.

"I'll get these to our lawyer first thing in the morning,"

Auntie Amethyst offered. "Now excuse me. I need a smoke before I cut a motherfucker."

She stormed out of the office without a backward glance.

Crystal rose to her feet and stood there on shaky legs, smiling benevolently at her sister. "For what it's worth, I think you're going to do a great job."

"You'll be here to tell me if I'm making mistakes," Lara pointed out. "Please, though, use words not noises like *hmmmmmmmm.*"

Her sister laughed but then shook her head. "I'm not going to be here. I told you that I'm ready to do the next thing, and part of that is... I met my mate."

Lara squealed with excitement then slapped Crystal on the arm. "Get out. How come you didn't tell me?"

"Sometimes people keep their mates secret because they have a good reason. Or at least *think* they have a good reason." Crystal grinned. "In my case, she's a cougar shifter from a clan based in Montana. She can't immigrate, so I'm moving south. I obviously couldn't say anything about leaving until we'd transferred power."

Lara glanced at Alex, her cheeks flushed, before turning back to Crystal. "I met her, didn't I? She delivered a note to me when I was at the spa."

"She likes you. You'll get a chance to meet her again soon, I promise. Now I need to go tell her what's up." Crystal tilted her head politely. "If that's okay with my Alpha?"

Lara breathed out a sigh that was satisfaction and exhaustion all at the same time. "It's okay with your *sister*, who loves you very much. Get out of here."

To Alex's immense shock, Crystal paused in front of

him, staring up at him with one brow raised. Assessing. Considering.

Sniffing, which made him roll his eyes.

She tossed a smirk at Lara then turned back and surprised him with a hug, squeezing tight before pounding him on the back as briskly as James or Cooper would've done.

"You're okay," Crystal declared before slipping from the room and unsteadily making her way down the hallway.

Wolves are weird, his bear stated. *Except ours.*

Alex snickered. *Hate to tell you this, but ours is weird too. But that's just fine.*

Because that weirdness was what made her unique and powerful. Made her exactly who he wanted to be with forever.

Becoming Alpha of the Orion pack wasn't the only change in Lara's future, because Alex intended to do whatever it took until she accepted *him* as well. They would end up together, as mates.

Permanent and perfect.

18

---

*I*t had been years since the Orion pack had changed leadership. Lara had been only eight when Crystal had taken over for the previous Alphas—their parents. She had few memories of that time, but it seemed there were enough old-timers and wolf instincts to make the transition not only seamless, but rapid.

An hour after their version of *Gunfight at the O.K. Corral*, Lara was staring around at her new living quarters in the pack house. It wasn't nearly as ostentatious as Shimmering Delights, but she did have a two-bedroom apartment with a private living room. The entire suite was on the main floor for easy access to all the pack mates, but it had been built to provide glorious views in three directions.

Lara stared out at the river, power still coursing through her veins.

Hands landed softly on her shoulders, stroking down her arms as Alex leaned against her back and pressed his cheek to hers. "You're damn near vibrating."

"I've never used that much power at one time," she confessed. "Normally I'd have been physically fighting at the same time, which would help burn off some of the adrenaline. I'm so twitchy I think caffeine would calm me down."

She pivoted on the spot and draped her arms around his neck.

He tapped their noses together. "You wolves are weird. Admit it."

While she agreed with him, she wasn't about to give him any more ammunition. "You meant to say wolves are brilliant, or at least my sister is."

"Okay, she's smart. But she's also lucky you were more dominant. The entire plan could've backfired."

"Maybe."

Except Alex didn't know there were a few tidbits she and Crystal had skimmed over. Although Crystal had come perilously close to spilling the beans when she'd mentioned mates.

Of course Crystal had known of the mate bond waiting between Lara and Alex. Lara mentally kicked her own butt for not having realized her Alpha would scent it, if nothing else.

When it came to the fight, Lara hadn't just been defending herself but righting a wrong for her pack and her mate. Or so she had believed. Crystal truly didn't want to stay in power, plus love for her mate was drawing her away.

The mysterious shifter power knew the best woman to be in charge was Lara. And mysterious powers were not to be trifled with.

But now it meant there were situations to be dealt with, including resetting her relationship with Alex. The sooner they started over, the sooner she'd be able to make a move and invite him into her life for real.

She cupped his face with her hands and patted his

cheeks gently. "First, thank you for what you did back there. For standing up with me yet letting me fight my own battle. That was..."

For some reason, her throat closed up as she fought to find the right words. It was amazing, and humbling, and made her wolf howl with longing to have him there all the time.

Lara took a deep breath and tried again. "Just, thank you."

His lips curled into a smile. "You're welcome, sugar."

She let her hands fall to her sides and stepped back. It was time, and prolonging it wasn't going to make the separation hurt any less. "The mystery is solved. Borealis Gems is safe, and you're done with the mating fever. I guess there's no reason for me to torment you and keep you at the pack house any longer."

The smile stayed, but the light in his eyes faded slightly. "You just got a bigger room, and a bigger bed. Seems a silly time to kick me out."

Oh God, this was going to be torture.

She tried again, but before she could get out more than a few fumbling words, Alex caught her by the hand and tugged her across the room to the couch that faced the wall of windows.

The sun had set a long time ago, but there were twinkling lights dancing along the water. Along the fence, a dozen hooks were arranged for pack members to leave their clothes, and even now, parts of her family were happily walking out and shifting to fur to run and hunt and enjoy life.

Howling rose on the air, happiness in the tone. It was the sound of a contented pack that knew they had a powerful Alpha in charge who cared for them and wanted their best.

God, it was the most wonderful moment of her life, and yet inside she was dying.

She needed her mate.

His big, beautiful head slipped between her and the scenery. Dark eyes examined her carefully. "I have something I want to tell you, and I need you to listen to all of it before you interrupt."

"That bad? *Interesting...*"

He snorted so hard he choked. Lara had to pat him on the back until he calmed down.

"On the list of things to talk about later, your Auntie Amethyst is a real number."

"She really is."

Alex caught Lara's fingers in his, staring at her hand as he rubbed his thumb over the back of her knuckles. "When I tracked you down because I had the mating fever, I swore the commitment was for the week and nothing more. I will stick to that promise because it's the right thing to do, and I know you're busy adjusting to being the new Alpha. I figured I should give you some time before I change anything up. I figured I would give you a couple of months before I asked you on a date, but then my bear had a different opinion—"

Oh my God. If she'd been able to suggest a solution, this would've been it. Lara pressed her fingers over his mouth to stop the words spewing out in a rapid stream. "You want to us to date? Starting in a couple of months?"

"*I* thought a couple of months, but my bear thinks we should start tomorrow. Hell, he kinda figured we should just keep on this instant, but I was trying to tell you that—"

Lara's wolf had perked up to full attention. *His bear is smart. Listen to bear. Let's do this now.*

Quiet, please, Lara said quickly. *Human side is in charge of timing, although I agree with you.*

Alex took a deep breath and squared his shoulders as if he were headed into battle. "Lara, I don't want to freak you out, and this isn't because of the mating fever, but damn, you're one hell of a woman. You're kind and considerate, and you can kick ass. Hell, you can kick *my* ass. I went into our time together impressed with you on one level, and I've come out the other end not sure how I can survive without you."

Words were slow to come. Her heart pounded so hard her entire body vibrated, and the power that she'd expended earlier in the day was like a tiny mote of dust compared to the pressure building inside her heart. "Me too. I mean, the way I feel about you changed over the past weeks. I've admired you, and I've wanted you, but now there's more to it. More layers. And it's not just because fate said it should be."

Alex breathed a sigh of relief. He dipped his chin firmly. "Then in a couple of weeks we can start dating."

Sweet, innocent, silly bear. Now that her wolf had gotten even an inkling that he was interested, he wasn't getting his furry butt out of her clutches. "Nope. Your timing sucks."

His eyes flared open. "Okay, then. A couple of months—"

She slid off the couch and landed in his lap, legs on either side of his hips. Her hands went to the top buttons of his shirt. "Your bear had the right idea. Not next week, not tomorrow, but now."

"Really?" Big hands grabbed her hips and held on as if he was never going to let go. "Oh, hell *yeah*."

She leaned forward to tell him the rest, but his lips caressed hers, soft and gentle. Ghosting smoothly with a tease that promised so much more.

He rose to his feet, still kissing her as he manoeuvred to the king-size bed. His shirt fell off his shoulders as she pushed it away, hands reaching down to work the button and zipper on his jeans.

Alex's hands were there as well, helping remove her clothing and tossing garments aside until he could crawl over her on the mattress, naked skin to naked skin.

He stopped, staring down at her, his dark eyes twinkling in the low light from the bedside table. He ran his fingers through her hair, spreading it out on the dark burgundy pillow. Then he shook his head, all muscles and firm strength pressed up against her gently, as if she were delicate.

"I was going to wait, but maybe my bear is right about this part as well."

His eyes—

Oh, his eyes were filled with wonder, and his expression was adoring, as if he were looking at a miracle.

"Lara? I love you."

A thrill shot through her so hard she felt it in every cell of her body. "Seriously?"

He stroked her cheek so tenderly. "No demands you say it back. Not until you're ready, but just so you know, I plan to work my ass off to make sure you feel the same—"

"You're my mate," she confessed. "My fated mate, as in, it's a wolf thing. I've known for months, but that's not the important part because I love you too."

Hopefulness mixed with confusion. "You've known I was your mate for months and you never said anything?"

She made a face. "We weren't exactly bosom buddies."

Alex looked horrified. He rolled off her and sat upright. "You knew we were mates when you handcuffed me to the handrail? I mean, when I was an idiot and tried to trick you into trusting me, and then you handcuffed me to the handrail as I so rightly deserved?"

"Yes, but could we get back to where we were a moment ago with you on top of me and us about to—"

Alex pinched the bridge of his nose and shook his head as if his brains were rattling around and he was trying to make them settle. Then he lifted his head sadly, hand reaching to grasp hers. "Now it makes sense. There were so many times I couldn't figure out what the hell was going on, and why you weren't just flattening my ass, but it was because you were trying not to burn bridges."

She fought to keep from smiling. "It's a little hard to try and convince someone you're worthy of forever when you've got them in a headlock on a regular basis."

"But that's not all, is it?" He scooped her up, and suddenly she was sitting in his lap naked, his fingers stroking delicately along her collarbone and down her shoulder and biceps. "I've heard stories. Knowing that I was your mate and not getting to be with me—God, that must've been killing you."

"I was pretty happy to share mating fever with you, even though it wasn't a forever thing," she admitted.

The heat rising in his eyes said it all. "I swear I'll make it up to you," he promised. "Every one of those months you spent in pain, I'll give you pleasure ten times over. For every month your wolf was lonely, I'll give you decades of companionship."

Accepted, her wolf shouted. *Signed, sealed, and delivered, please.*

Lara giggled.

Alex raised a brow.

She pressed her hand to his chest and wiggled in close. "My wolf would like to know if we could consummate that proposal with a bit more than a handshake."

"With pleasure."

He took control and proceeded to kiss every inch of her body, sliding over the mattress and adjusting her as he pleased until she was quivering with need and trembling on the edge of the precipice.

Of course, that's when he pulled back, eyes widening as he stared down at her where he had her pinned, his cock hovering at the entrance to her sex. "I just realized something."

Lara shrieked, pounding her fists on his shoulders. "Oh my God, I'm going to kill you. Sex now, revelations later."

"No, this is important," Alex insisted. "You see, during the mating fever, you already knew we were mates. So did your wolf and my bear, which means that whole *everybody needs to be on board* thing? The only holdout keeping us from becoming full mates was *me*."

She hadn't thought of it that way. "And...?"

A steady forward thrust of his hips brought his cock into contact, and as he slipped into her body, something magical happened.

Perfection wrapped tight, comfortable and yet binding in a way that she knew meant never being lonely or separated, no matter the distance between them. Pleasure streaked up her spine, radiating into her limbs and tingling up the back of her head.

"When James and Kaylee went through the mating

fever, he accepted it and felt the possibility of it right away, but she didn't. It wasn't until she accepted the bond that it came into being." Alex was moving in her now, joined intimately as he leaned his lips next to her ear and whispered. "I choose you. I want you. I *love* you."

"I love you too—"

He notched his mouth against the curve of her shoulder. A sharp pain seared through her as he bit down. Words vanished and a blinding light filled the room. *Oh my God, this is really happening.*

Alex groaned, hips pumping until he came as well. Spine arching, a cry of fulfillment on his lips. He lowered himself gently, their chests still heaving and bodies shaking with satisfaction.

Lara couldn't hold back any longer. *"Please tell me you can hear this,"* she thought at Alex.

He jerked upright, staring at her in astonishment. *"Lara?"*

Hearing her name in her head, spoken with every nuance of his tone and absolute wonder, was the cherry on top. She wrapped her arms around him and used momentum to flip them so that he was flat on his back and she knelt on top. Then she thrust her arms into the air and squealed with happiness.

A second later, she clapped her hands to his chest and again spoke the way that mated wolves did. Private, and intimate, and oh so perfect. *"Looks as if we're mated, sweetie."*

His smile was huge, his happiness clear. *"Which means you're stuck with me."*

She laughed, the sound rising and growing stronger as she realized what else this meant. "Looks as if a few others are stuck with you, as well," she pointed out. "Welcome to the Orion pack, Alex Borealis."

Joy filled every part of her as his expression morphed into shock as Alex realized exactly what fate had signed him up for.

He got to deal with wolves from now until forever.

19

*I*n the spirit of cooperation, they held their mating celebration at the high school. The wolves provided the food, the bears brought the alcohol. The local authorities agreed to turn a blind eye to any shenanigans as long as everyone stayed off the roads, which seemed a completely reasonable request as far as Alex was concerned.

They'd waited a month to let things settle down a little, and winter had arrived in Yellowknife. The October wind blew cool across the snowdrifts, but inside the school gymnasium, it was warm and cozy, the scent of good food lingering in the air.

The feel of his arm around Lara's waist was pretty damn perfect. He'd taken to coming up behind her wherever she stood and silently joining her as she chatted with the pack or communicated with people from the diamond mines. He didn't need to be front and center, but the part that made him feel a million miles tall was how she'd ease slightly closer, settling against him and relaxing as if she didn't need to worry about pulling out her bad-assery when he was around.

Although she still did, moving like a lightning bolt when it was required by the pack, because his ninja warrior woman was awesome to the core.

He did it now, walking forward and slipping into position as Lara chatted with Auntie Amethyst. Today the older woman's outfit was fluorescent orange with bold splashes of purple. It would've looked fantastic with her dyed hair, except she gotten that redone so it was now a brilliant red that clashed with her orange scarf.

It was enough to make a bear go blind, but Lara had relaxed back against him, so everything was right in his world.

He acknowledged Amethyst politely. "Auntie. You're looking particularly fine today."

The older woman sniffed delicately then cracked a smile. "Go on with ya, mischief-maker. You bought the clothes for me, and you know it."

Lara glanced at him in surprise. "You did?"

He grinned at having pulled one over on her. "I did. A gift in exchange for a promise." He held out a hand to Auntie. "Show me."

She gave him her wrist and pushed up the fitted sleeve of her jacket to show the nicotine patches decorating her arm. "Wolf metabolism being what it is, I hope you know I've got the chemist down at the Shoppers Drug Mart horrified by my recent bulk purchases."

He leaned in and offered her a kiss on the cheek. The scent of stale smoke had vanished, leaving a far more pleasant aroma like the wind across the snow in its place. "Enjoy yourself tonight, Auntie. But be careful around that one." He pointed across the room to an elderly gentleman who was tapping the floor with his cane and smiling eagerly at all the single women walking past. "He's a bit of a charmer."

Auntie Amethyst straightened, quickly replacing her eager hunter enthusiasm with nonchalance. "Well, I'd hate to have anybody bored at your party. Later, gators."

She vanished.

Lara linked her fingers with his as they sauntered toward a different corner of the room. "*Please tell me you didn't sic her on somebody defenceless.*"

Being able to respond through their mate connection instead of whispering was so amazing. "*Old man Jenner is a grizzly nearly my size. Trust me, he can take care of himself.*"

They pulled to a stop beside where Crystal and her mate were chatting with Gramps and Grandma. It had taken a while, but his bear was no longer completely offended at the old man's rude behaviour and comments about Lara.

Crystal and Chantelle were so in love, it was wonderful to see.

Lara laid a hand on her sister's shoulder. "You two are staying for a few days, yes?"

Crystal nodded. "It'll be nice to spend time at the pack house without having to sneak around so nobody spots us."

"We can stay for a week, then I have to get back to work. But you're all welcome to come and visit us any time," Chantelle offered. Her dark hair was pulled back into a puffy ponytail, and she twisted on her chair to face Grandma Laureen. "My clan owns plenty of land, and if you come in the winter you can ski. If you come in the summer, we've got lots of beautiful areas for running. Plus, we're going to open a spa next year, if you're interested, Mrs. Borealis."

Alex's grandmother nodded enthusiastically. "I'm not

much of a skier, but I like hot tubs, and running, and definitely the spa. Giles and I will be gone in a few weeks to the spa in this area. I don't know if you've heard of it. Shimmering Delights?"

Chantelle smiled. "It might have been mentioned a time or two."

Grandma Laureen sighed happily. "We have an entire week booked. I had hoped we'd be able to get away back in August, but Giles had to cancel our reservation at the last minute. The Grand Salon is so wonderful. And the food is fantastic."

Gramps was suddenly looking everywhere except at Alex and Lara. Fidgeting as if his change of demeanour would make him invisible. "Well, look at that," he said pointing across the room.

"You had a reservation in August?" Lara spoke sweetly, but she'd obviously picked up on what had caught Alex's attention as well. "How disappointing that you had to postpone your trip."

Grandma waved it off before poking Gramps in the arm. "Stop fidgeting like you're a two-year-old. I don't know why he gets like this sometimes," she said conspiratorially to them, right in front of his face. "It's as if he gets so distracted he simply can't concentrate for longer than a couple minutes. I think I need to increase his doses of leafy green vegetables. Brain food, you know."

Alex laughed out loud. "Definitely. I hear kale and spinach are fantastic for memory."

"Your grandfather hates kale," Lara shared with amusement before speaking out loud and adding a nail to the coffin. "Brussel sprouts as well, Grandma Laureen. Very important. He should have large servings of those vegetables."

Alex squeezed Lara's waist then made their excuses, pulling her away and walking briskly into the hallway.

They barely made it into the more private location before breaking out into gales of laughter.

"Oh my God, the only thing Gramps hates more than kale are Brussels sprouts."

Lara wiped away her tears. "I know. And maybe that was a little mean, but oh my God, it was *him*. He somehow manoeuvred to get me up to the spa."

"You don't know the half of it. I had snuck into the pack house and found out the information about you going to the spa, but he didn't know that. That's why he called and set me on your tracks when I was coming down with the fever."

Lara blinked. Her amusement fading slightly as confusion rolled in. Then she smacked him on the arm briskly. "Alex Borealis, you snuck into the pack house? What kind of move was that?"

"A brilliant one?" he offered. She continued to glare. "Hey, don't give me that look. I successfully snuck in and out without any of your wolves catching me. I think that probably means I've got the upper hand when it comes to the question of who's better at security."

She wrinkled her nose.

"I promise I won't gloat." He stole a quick kiss. "I won't gloat too much," he amended.

A sharp snicker escaped her, but Lara wrapped her fingers around his arm, and they marched back into the gymnasium.

"There they are."

"Guests of honour need to get into position."

"Hurry up, we want to see the show."

Alex escorted Lara through the eager gathering of

wolves, settling her in one of the folding chairs that waited front and center festooned with balloons and streamers.

His brother James came forward and draped a sash around his neck. "Figured you'd need something special to identify you."

Alex glanced down. There was an arrow pointing to one side above the words *Mated to this Beautiful Woman*. "It's awesome, bro. I'll wear it proudly."

His brother finished placing one over Lara's head then stepped back. Way back, far enough that it was impossible to smack him as Alex read the words on Lara's sash. *I'm Stuck with Him.*

He glared at his brother. "Be careful or I will use my superior sleuthing skills to find out what pet names your mate calls you, and I will do something devastating with that info."

Kaylee shouted from a few rows away. "Is my cute furry baby bothering you, Alex?"

"There you go. Superior sleuthing skills achieved." Lara leaned over the back of her chair and pointed a finger at her sister-in-law. "They *are* cute. You mean when they're in their polar bear forms, right?"

"Totally. I mean, they're big and impressive, but so gosh darn cute. I just want to snuggle him all the time."

Alex exchanged glances with his brother, both of them sighing heavily. "So much for us being the most feared predators of the north."

James shrugged. "I suppose it's better this way. More snuggles."

Brisk clapping sounded from the side as Auntie Amethyst marched forward, leaving the older gentleman bear she'd been canoodling with grinning happily in the background. "Okay, kids, gather around. We've got some home movies that we thought would be appropriate for today's party."

Chairs were scuffled and voices lowered as the motley crew settled into position.

Alex linked his fingers with Lara's, arm curled around her shoulders to keep her close. "Family movies. You realize if I see any signs of you lying on a bearskin rug, I'm going to be very put out."

Laughter rose from the pack, but Lara was the one who spoke quietly into his mind. *"I seem to remember lying on a bear's skin lately. Very naked."*

Damn. He shouldn't have said anything. Now he was going to be uncomfortable for the rest of the evening until he could convince her it was time for them to go back to their private quarters.

Or maybe he could convince her that they should check out the broom closet there at the school.

Someone dimmed the lights and queued up a Bluetooth connection. Just as the projector started, Mac the cat prowled by, sliding in front of the light to create an enormous monstrous shadow on the screen.

The wolves howled and the bears clapped. Mac glared at them haughtily before slowly, very slowly, pacing off.

The background to the video was music with a catchy beat, and Alex was tapping his toes before he realized what was happening on the screen in front of him.

It was him sauntering up to Lara. He was dressed head to toe in black and she was holding Mac, and within a few moments he realized he was watching video footage of their meeting outside the school.

Parts moved in fast-forward, but every detail of the most important moments were played out or repeated in slow motion.

When Lara flipped him and slammed him into the ground, there was a collective *ohhhhhh* from the gathered wolves and a "you go girl" from Amber.

And that wasn't the end. The next scene was a shot of Lara in the pack house, happiness in her expression as she jotted down a note and left it on the desk. Then she was alert, moving like the ninja she was toward the door. The screen split, and suddenly she was on one side, sliding like a ghost toward where a shadow lay on the floor. The other half showed him, back against the wall, inching his way toward where she would inevitably find him.

The screen split again, this time, the third video showing the common room of the pack house with Auntie Amethyst sitting in her recliner, a large bowl of popcorn in her lap. She was watching them both on *her* television. When it became clear that Lara was closing in on discovering him, Auntie rolled her eyes then deliberately held her popcorn bowl to one side before letting it go, cupping her hands to her mouth and shouting for help.

Lara straightened instantly and took off at a run, vanishing out of the picture and reappearing in the common room to help with cleanup.

Meanwhile Alex had slipped into the office and found his information.

He sighed heavily as the camera followed him all the way back down the hallway, up into the attic, and away from the pack house.

"So much for being a super sleuth," he said wryly.

Lara snorted. "They got me too," she pointed out.

Her grip on his fingers tightened, and he really didn't care that he'd been caught on camera because, in the end, what they had together was more important.

Besides, they had gotten to the truly interesting part of

the video. This one involved a lot more nighttime shots, but it was pretty clear that there was a bear wandering the pack house in the dead of night.

A polar bear sitting at the pack computer and carefully using one long nail to punch in orders on...Amazon?

Lara leaned against him. "What are you doing?"

"Not sure," he admitted. "Give me a second."

What were you doing? he asked his bear.

Wooing. I told you I would take care of things, his inner beast said proudly.

And while online shopping was the source for some of the gifts, it was Alex in bear form who hauled in the lake trout, awkwardly dragging an overloaded bag across the floor until stopped by—of all people—Crystal.

She shook her head in amusement before hauling a kiddie pool out of the storage closet. She helped him deposit his gift then snuck him back into Lara's room.

It seemed there'd been more than a few people conspiring to get them together.

A collective sigh of happiness went up from the wolf pack, and Lara turned to him with love in her eyes. "*Awww.* The gifts were from you all along."

"I guess so," he admitted. "I should give my bear credit."

"Then he is quite the charmer." There was more video playing from the time after Lara and Crystal's fight, the days when Alex had begun to get to know the pack members, playing games and talking and hanging out in the evenings.

It was entertaining to watch, and it made something glow in Alex's heart. He had a new place in the world. Not only at Lara's side, but in the midst of a wild and unruly pack of wolves.

Not bad for a straitlaced security expert.

Not bad for someone who'd been planning to avoid mating fever at all costs.

He took the glass of whiskey his brother offered him, staring down at the amber fluid that reminded him so much of the highlights in his mate's eyes. The sweet scent rose to his nostrils, and he looked across the room to find Gramps staring at him, a satisfied smirk on the old man's face.

He'd been manipulative, and yet it had been exactly what Alex needed to light a fire under him.

He raised his glass to the old man. "I'll admit it. You were right. Thank you."

Grandfather Giles grinned and lifted his glass in return. "I figured you'd see things my way. That's why I was nice and didn't offer up the Canada Day security footage of you in that staircase for the show."

Alex choked on his whiskey. "No way."

Gramps tilted his head slightly, his expression one step away from full-out grin. "To your happily mated future."

Alex didn't know if he should laugh or scream. The old man was incredible. At some point Alex wanted to grow up to be as sneaky as him.

"*Does this mean I don't get to chastise him anytime soon?*" Lara asked dryly.

"*You can go ahead and offer my grandmother all the suggestions you want to get him force fed more vegetables, but I think we'll keep him unharmed for a while. Grandma likes him, and he's kind of amusing.*"

Lara pulled Alex to his feet, gesturing with a hand as the chairs were pulled out of the way and the music started, and the two of them danced.

She rested her head against his chest, sighing contentedly. "I love you, Alex Borealis. Thanks for stepping into my world."

"I love you, Lara Lazuli. Thanks for trusting this grumpy bear with your heart."

"Always and forever."

Which was, Alex realized, exactly the way it was supposed to be. *"My fated mate."*

EPILOGUE

*A*mber sat next to her friends, laughing at one of their jokes before sliding off the bench and accepting the invitation from another wolf for a dance.

The entire evening she'd wondered exactly how to go about what she needed to do. It seemed an appropriate moment—a celebration where two very different individuals were showcasing their ability to join together and make their lives even better.

Watching her friend Kaylee fall in love and become mated to James had been a bit of a miracle in Amber's books. Not because she didn't think Kaylee deserved such happiness, but because being up close and personal watching someone fall in love hadn't been a big part of Amber's past experiences.

Her world had been very small, with her brother her only real family for the past couple years. When he'd gone missing, she'd been devastated. Being accepted into the Borealis family the way she had was so meaningful.

And now she stared with deep emotion as grumbly Alex teased his mate until Lara effortlessly flipped him to the ground. She stood with one four-inch heel pressed against his sternum, baring her teeth until he held up his hands in mock surrender and begged for mercy—

Something warm and fuzzy that could only be called joy rumbled around in Amber's chest.

A hand rested on her shoulder briefly. "You okay?"

Amber stared into Cooper's piercing blue eyes, the silver-tipped highlights in his hair reflecting the colours dancing off the disco ball in the corner of the room. Was she okay? She would be doing fantastic if she could get up the courage to tell a certain someone that she was feeling all sorts of very non-coworker-y emotions for him.

Although, was he really a coworker when he was her boss?

She fought a sigh and instead pasted on a big smile. "It's a fantastic party. I'm so happy for your brother. *Brothers*—" She twisted to include James in her comment as he twirled past, Kaylee on his arm. The two of them were spinning faster than was probably safe in the crowded space.

Cooper settled in the chair beside her, his gaze on the dance floor. "They've been very fortunate. It's been a good year."

The music thumped on, and Amber pressed her heels against the ground to keep from tapping in time. Then she reconsidered because this was potentially the perfect opportunity for her to take a stand.

To somehow let Cooper Borealis know that, while she was only human, and yes, his secretary, surely there was *some* way they could work around those technical difficulties because he really was the most attractive man she'd ever seen in her life.

But more than that, he did something to her heart. Inside, where that connection to family and friends longed to be filled. Cooper's gentleness called to her, and while it might not be the easiest relationship to figure out, she thought it would be worth it.

Amber took a deep breath, screwed up her courage, and then turned to blurt out, "Would you like to dance?"

She was talking to empty air.

Silently—impossibly silent considering the size of the man—he'd risen from her side and was already a dozen paces across the room. His broad shoulders swayed slowly, the lazy animal flair of his bear showing up in his human stride.

Sexy man. Annoying, frustrating, irritating, sexy man.

Every time she worked up the courage to say something, it was as if his radar pinged and he disappeared. It wasn't right.

It was frustrating as hell.

Amber Myawayan folded her arms over her chest and examined the room more thoroughly. There were wolves and bears and cougars and bobcats, some in their shifted forms and some dressed to the teeth as humans. All of them celebrating. All of them enjoying life to the fullest.

Now on the far side of the gymnasium, shoulders pressed against the wall, Cooper stared into space. Frustration in his expression, his shoulders drooped. The farthest thing from a man filled with delight and happiness.

He *was* happy for his brothers, but the same way she felt a missing piece inside while watching her friends find lovers to share their days and nights with, Cooper had to be hurting. Had to be lonely.

That was when Amber came to the sudden and wonderful realization that she didn't need to be afraid anymore. If this was meant to be, then there was plenty of opportunity for her to turn the tables on her gallant bear.

Plenty of people who would help her as well...

After two years in the north, she'd learned that, as well. Maybe it wasn't the way things were done in the human world, but she was obviously working with different dynamics when it came to shifters, and especially polar bear shifters.

Amber rose to her feet, straightened her skirt, and stepped carefully across the gymnasium floor to where another powerhouse sat.

Grandma Laureen was out on the dance floor with Alex, so Amber slid into the empty seat beside the family patriarch, turning to him as nonchalantly as possible. Her heart pounded even as she offered a shy smile.

Grandfather Giles raised a brow, his grin slowly widening as he examined her face. "Hello, Amber. You look as if there's something on your mind."

It was her last chance to turn back, to pretend as if this wasn't why she'd made her way over here, but she wanted Cooper far too much to lie. Human or not, job complications or not, they *both* deserved to be happy. They both deserved to see if being together would help them find that happiness.

She gathered her courage then boldly answered. "There's something I would very much like your help with."

~

New York Times Bestselling Author Vivian Arend
brings you a light-hearted paranormal trilogy
Borealis Bears

Get mated—or else!

When the meddling, match-making family patriarch lays
down the law, Giles Borealis' three polar bear shifter
grandsons agree to follow his edict. Only James, Alex and
Cooper each have a vastly different plan in mind to deal
with their impending mating fevers. Will any of them be
able to fight fate?

Spoiler: *not likely!*

~

Borealis Bears
The Bear's Chosen Mate
The Bear's Fated Mate
The Bear's Forever Mate

~

ABOUT THE AUTHOR

With over 2 million books sold, Vivian Arend is a *New York Times* and *USA Today* bestselling author of over 50 contemporary and paranormal romance books, including the Six Pack Ranch and Granite Lake Wolves.

Her books are all standalone reads with no cliffhangers. They're humorous yet emotional, with sexy-times and happily-ever-afters. Vivian pretty much thinks she's got the best job in the world, and she's looking forward to giving readers more HEAs. She lives in B.C. Canada with her husband of many years and a fluffy attack Shih-tzu named Luna who ignores everyone except when treats are deployed.

www.vivianarend.com

CPSIA information can be obtained
at www.ICGtesting.com
Printed in the USA
LVHW111600081119
636787LV00004B/747/P